THE FIRE CHRONICLES

Whispers of the Dragon

Leigha Acosta

Great Many Thanks to My Family.

To My Readers:

You know that one thing you've always wanted to do or be?

Well, what's stopping you?

You can do anything you put your mind to.

Acknowledgment

Special Thanks to:

My mom, who spent hours every day working on proofreading my book. Thank you for spending SO much time and effort helping me with this book. I am very grateful that you did this for me. I know that it was nerve-racking for both of us! Thank you so much for striving to make this book the best it could be. □

❄❄❄

My editor Hezron Smith who gave us all the information and insights. Thank you for all the help! Very grateful you've been willing to help and have been cooperative. Thank you for understanding everything we needed from day one and answering every question we had.

Prologue

"Gaīa. The earth is crying for help," said a hushed, angelic voice. Several voices echoed concern.

"Yes, Aodh. We hear, and we will answer its calls," answered Gaīa, as she placed her wing on Aodh's shoulder in comfort.

"Tell Nēra we have a plan," said Sôl when he came up beside Gaīa.

"Selfīna, show them the way," said Gaīa as she looked at the blind dragon that lay in the corner. The dragon nodded, stood, and slipped out of the cave and into the dark.

"The time has come," bellowed Selfīna. As a response, water droplets fell from the ceiling of the cave, and calls of peace erupted from the gathered council of dragons. All the remaining dragons stared at the golden egg with admiration.

Contents

PART IV WINTER'S BEGINNING

PART V BEGINNING OF FIRE AND WATER

PART I
SUMMER, ORINSHIRE

Chapter I

Drea & Khan

"Hey, get away. Away with you. Guards!" the heavyset vendor bellowed. Drea cried out in pain as she was thrown to the ground, the rough stone scraping her elbows and palms. All she took was a small, bruised apple. It's not likely to have been bought anyway. The fact that the fruit was a little scarce in the kingdom might have had something to do with it.

Times were hard, and the oppression was real. Orinshire was not what it used to be. She heard that the Great King Dolion had sent his army to this place because of the dragons, but Drea thought it was poppycock. Dragons were just myths to scare the townspeople into submission. Never in her life had she seen or heard rumors of dragons being near Orinshire.

The soldiers were always watching, executing, and imprisoning those who did not support the King's rule. A rough hand quickly took hold of her arm and hoisted her up, pulling her away from her thoughts.

"Sorry, sir. She's not quite there yet, in 'er mind, sir. I'll take care of 'er. No, no need for those," said an oddly familiar voice.

Drea fought against the hand that held tight to her upper arm as she was pulled away from the vendor. Then, someone grabbed her from behind and tossed her into an alley, making her head spin. Drea's thick black hair fell over her face, partially obscuring her view of her assailant. She pulled her hair away from her eyes with a scraped-up hand so she could see better. It was her twin brother, Khan. She wasn't surprised, but she was grateful.

Drea got up off the ground and looked Khan in the eye. His face was a mask of concern, laced with anger. Khan pushed her further into the alley. "Do you have any idea what you just pulled?" Khan shouted, throwing his hands up in the air.

Drea bit her lip and looked at her feet. She hated it when her brother got angry with her. "Now, people are going to be on the lookout for you. If you try to steal something, the vendors will recognize you and take you away! What will I do then?"

"Did you even think?" continued Khan.

Drea let out a shaky sigh as Khan wrapped his arms around her and pulled her into a tight hug. Just as her head touched his shoulder, she heard a small, ghostly whisper echo in her mind.

"Once, twice, thrice. The wings of war shall sound."

Khan looked at her, his golden-green eyes showing concern.

"What? What is it?" Khan asked, shaking Drea to get her attention. Drea drew away, shaking her head, as a bad headache took hold of her mind. Unable to think or clear her mind, she slowly dropped into a crouched position and sat with her knees to her chest. Khan knelt in front of her, his hands on her shoulders to steady himself. Visions clouded her sight—*there was a dragon chasing a man on a cliff, something fell. She couldn't tell what it was. The last thing she saw was the sea by a cluster of cliffs.*

❄❄❄

Khan watched his twin sleep with anxiety. Her seizures appeared to be getting worse. They lived in a small abandoned basement, a tiny fire lit up the room from inside a small fireplace. A small, white cat cuddled next to his leg, its thick, bushy tail curled around its muzzle.

Not that long ago, the same thing had happened to Khan. Except he saw a small gold and white egg laying at the bottom of a water-filled cave. Drea had told him what she saw; Khan dismissed it, though it connected with his vision. He didn't like to refer to them as 'visions.' They were more like daydreams that invaded his and his sister's minds whenever they got the chance.

The waning moon shone directly above Drea's position. The small, broken window allowed the light of the moon to illuminate Drea's face. Time seemed to slow as muffled wing beats and battle cries echoed in his ears. A blue dragon obscured Khan's vision as it flew out of the sea.

Its wings spread wide as it roared at the world and flew toward the shore. Something small and gold was clutched in its front talons. A larger white dragon with tinged blue scales followed swiftly behind the blue one.

Its massive jaws were thrown open as white dust fumed out of its mouth and into the air behind the blue dragon's tail. The blue dragon roared as the dust touched its tail and froze the tip of it.

Khan shut his eyes as he rubbed them. He didn't believe in the dragons. He was sure many others didn't either. However, the elders told Khan that when they were children, dragons and mankind used to live side-by-side as one. Khan just thought that these were bedtime stories and myths that kept children in their beds at night. He shook his head and closed his eyes.

❄❄❄

Drea woke up with a start. Her eyes scanned the room. This room looked nothing like the one she was in before. Panicked, she stood and ran around the room, searching for ways out.

"Help! Help me! Someone?" Drea cried into the darkness.

“Shh! You’ll make them come back!” a voice behind her instantly whispered.

Drea squinted into the darkness and could only make out the blonde color of her twin brother’s hair. She stifled a scream as Khan’s hand shot out and tugged her into the darkness.

“Who—”

Khan slapped a hand over Drea’s mouth before she could finish and held a finger to his lips as footsteps slowly walked overhead. Something fuzzy skimmed Drea’s jaw. She turned to see Ariela, the white female cat who lived with them, her eyes wide and scared as the footsteps stopped directly above them. Drea gazed up through the small peephole in one of the wooden floorboards. She held her breath as a man’s face came into view. He had harsh features with black hair and cold gray eyes.

“Torch the place!” growled the man before he was handed a torch.

“They’re likely dead anyway,” the man continued as he threw the torch into the old and broken furniture.

Fear took hold of Drea’s heart as the crackle of fire and the smell of smoke flowed down to the place where they hid. Khan held onto Drea’s hand as if it were the only thing keeping him planted on the stone of the basement.

Khan and Drea escaped out of the basement after the men were gone.

“Come on.” He said while he pulled her toward a sewer entrance. Khan dragged his twin through tunnels, swinging this way and that as Drea held fiercely onto the cat. No way were they going to leave the poor thing to fend for itself in the fire.

Khan skidded to a halt as another series of tunnels stretched out before him. He groaned as he decided which one to choose. One tunnel stood out to him—a small dot of light shone at the end of it. "This way!"

As Drea charged after her brother, her left foot slammed against a lift in the sewer floor. She screamed and fell forward into the dirty, smelly water. Ariela went flying from her arms. She screamed for Khan, but he was already out of range. The water began pulling her away.

❄❄❄

Khan stepped out of the sewer back into the light above ground, unaware that his sister was not behind him. He turned and jumped as Ariela came bounding past him. With heart pounding, he stared back into the sewage pipe. He couldn't see anything in the tunnel.

He glanced around. There must be someone here who would help. He grabbed Ariela and started toward the marketplace.

❄❄❄

Drea slowly pulled herself out of the murky water and onto a dirty embankment. The air was thick around the water, and the smell of bugs, and dead fish was heavy on the wind.

After pulling herself up onto the embankment, she sat down and looked around. Khan was nowhere to be seen. She panicked.

Drea stood and searched the water, yelling Khan's name. Just then, a hand appeared in the waterline and opened as if begging for help.

"Khan!" Drea gasped as she waded her way back into the dirty water. She reached for the hand, but it disappeared and was replaced with hundreds of pointed teeth. She screamed and thundered through the water back to the bank. The water behind her erupted into a giant splash as a large creature broke through the surface and quickly followed her. Drea drew a large breath and dove into the dirty water to swim faster. Her breath caught in her throat as the creature took hold of her ankle and started spinning her in the water. She screamed, the pain was like nothing she'd ever felt before. Drea grabbed at her throat, the air in her body beginning to depart and suffocate her.

The last thing she saw before blackness enclosed her was a pair of hands grabbing at the creature.

❄❄❄

Khan watched with fear as the man he had asked for help pounded on Drea's chest to get the water out of her lungs. Khan's eyes were drawn to her right ankle—it was torn and bloodied. He had forgotten about Ariela who was now paddling out of the water and up onto the shore. Khan had dropped her into the water when he saw that the crocodile had a hold of his sister.

"It's. Not. Working," the man cried, drawing Khan's attention to Drea.

Khan jumped up and ran over to the man and Drea. He was still trying to force the water out of her lungs, but not one drop came out of Drea's mouth. Tears welled in Khan's eyes as the man continued pushing on her chest. The man, out of instinct, shoved Khan away and covered Drea from his sight. Khan couldn't believe it. His heart ached as he begged the One above to allow him to keep his sister for a little while longer. Khan tried to stifle the sobs that escaped his throat as the man began to scream at Drea, trying to shake her awake. Though now, he knew there wasn't much of a chance.

"Come back to me," Khan whispered.

He closed his eyes, covered his ears, and rocked back and forth like a baby in a cradle. After what seemed like an eternity, the sound of a triumphant yell broke through the barrier of his covered ears and caused him to open his eyes and look up. Drea was on her side, vomiting up the water she had swallowed.

Khan let out a stifled sob of relief and crawled over to Drea. He was relieved but exhausted by the anxiety of the last three minutes he just endured. The man moved away rigidly and sat on the ground before collapsing onto his back, breathing as though the weight of the world was on top of his chest.

As Drea came to her senses, she recoiled from the place where she had just vomited up the water. Khan drew her into a soft hug. The man who had helped Drea was walking toward them. He knelt on the ground and gently pushed Khan away. He then carefully reached down, picked Drea up as if she weighed nothing at all, and stood up with no apparent difficulty.

Khan grabbed Ariela and gently placed the filthy white cat on his sister's stomach as the man carried her. With some difficulty, Drea opened her eyes and smiled as she stroked the she-cat's dirty fur.

❄❄❄

Drea listened to the conversation between her brother and the stranger. The man's name was Lukas. He was taking them back to his cabin, some distance from the swamp, much to Drea's relief. The thing that had attacked her was a 'crocodile.' Lukas seemed to know everything about everything. She could tell that Khan enjoyed the man's company, even if he was a stranger.

Drea, however, felt it unnecessary for the man to help them now that the danger was past. What was in it for him? Khan seemed to get along with Lukas very well, much to Drea's surprise. She glanced up at her rescuer. His features were sharp, his hair a deep black, and he had dark-brown, kind-looking eyes. His thick, black beard was streaked with gentle wisps of gray. There was a long scar that traveled from his chin down to the collar of his shirt.

Though she was still groggy from the whole ordeal, she couldn't help but wonder how he acquired such a scar. Her attention was drawn back to Khan as she heard him begin to speak to the man once again. The man continued to talk with him, obviously happy to have some company.

A small dog came toward them, causing Ariela to hiss and arch her back.

"Ho, Gael!" yelled Lukas, pushing the dog away. The dog was clearly curious about the newcomers.

Drea drew away from the dog. It was easily the size of a small wolf. It had dark brown fur with spots of red. The dog jumped up once more. This time, it touched Drea's injured ankle with its heavy muzzle. Her ankle was still throbbing and that didn't help.

"Down!" Lukas shouted.

The dog instantly recoiled, whining as it followed slowly behind Khan.

They were approaching Lukas's house. He carried her up the porch steps and stopped at the door. Drea held tight to Ariela. Lukas leaned down and angled himself just enough to allow Drea to put a foot down on the step. Khan took hold of her arm and steadied her as Lukas opened the door to his home. He quickly took hold of Drea's other arm when she stumbled. The two lifted her off the ground and into the house. A small couch and an oversized chair occupied a cozy space near the hearth where a small fire burned.

"Grab that chair over there, will you?" Lukas asked.

Lukas took Drea's full weight and Khan let go and rushed over to a small wooden chair. Lukas slowly helped Drea onto the couch and propped her leg up with the wooden chair.

Khan watched Lukas stitch up Drea's ankle with a thin needle and string. He had given Drea a sleeping draught so she wouldn't feel pain every time the needle went through her skin. Khan didn't even need to explain what had happened—he just told Lukas he had lost his sister and needed help to find her. Lukas handled Drea with care that Khan had never seen before. The dog, Gael, sat beside an annoyed Ariela. Even the dog seemed to be concerned about Drea. His thoughts returned to Lukas, and he decided he should thank the man.

"Thank you," Khan said awkwardly, rubbing his hands together slowly.

Lukas looked at him momentarily then nodded and went back to his work.

Chapter II

The Visitors

Early in the afternoon, three days after Drea and Khan had arrived at Lukas's cabin, Drea sat in a rickety wooden chair outside on the front porch. She watched with amusement while Khan shouted at the fluffy, white sheep in the yard, waving a big staff in the air. Her attention was drawn to Lukas who was working a little farther away tending to a beautiful bay stallion. He held a medium-sized brush in his left hand and the lead rope in the other. Lukas brushed the stallion's coat until it shined.

Drea had already finished her chores, though there weren't many. Mostly sweeping and cleaning. She still wasn't able to do much. The crocodile had torn up her ankle much worse than she originally thought. She still wasn't able to move some of her toes.

"Hey, Drea!" Called Lukas.

She withdrew from her thoughts and looked toward him. "Come help me put Rán in the barn, would you?"

Drea shook her head as a smile spread across her face. She slowly stood, took hold of her thick cane and hobbled over to Lukas and the horse, Rán. The large stallion stared at her with gentle brown eyes. She tenderly put her hand on his warm muzzle and laughed as she felt Rán blow out a hot puff of air through his nostrils.

Drea let out a small grunt as Lukas gripped her waist and hoisted her up onto Rán's bare back.

"Uh, are you sure?" Drea asked, heart pounding a little faster.

Lukas nodded and gripped the horse's reins. He walked Rán in a wide circle, allowing him to get used to Drea's weight. Drea grabbed a handful of the horse's long dark mane and pressed her knees into Rán's sides so she wouldn't slide off. Rán tossed his head up and down, finishing with a loud neigh. Lukas smiled and laughed.

"Think he likes you!"

Drea held tight as Lukas slowly led Rán around the perimeter of the farm. She laughed and giggled as Khan gaped up at her. His face had a look bordering on jealousy.

"How come she gets a free ride while I have to do chores?" Complained Khan as he jogged up to Lukas's side.

Lukas shook his head, then smiled and helped Khan onto Rán's back right behind Drea.

"How come you get the front?" Grumbled Khan as he held onto her waist while Rán plodded on.

❄❄❄

The next morning, Khan and Lukas had left the cabin quite early, careful not to wake Drea. They needed to go back into Orinshire. Khan had left a note for Drea in case she woke up before they got back. He was scared to leave her on her own, especially after what had happened.

Khan was careful not to show his face openly. Lukas said they needed supplies and he wanted Khan and Drea to have a new set of clothes. The clothes he wore now would surely be considered rags. He stayed close to Lukas as they walked down the vendor's market row. As they continued on, a faint drizzle of rain started just as they entered the clothing shop.

Lukas seemed to be anxious as Khan sorted through the clothes. They had already gotten all the other supplies. *What was he so worried about?* Khan wondered. Maybe he just wanted to get back before the weather got any worse? Khan picked out a dark blue tunic and leather pants for Drea and a dark red tunic and black leather pants for himself. As he handed the clothes to Lukas, Lukas handed him two pairs of brown boots. Both were a good size for himself and Drea.

Lukas nodded as he handed over a few pieces of golden coins to the shop manager.

"Come on, we better get back."

❄❄❄

Drea woke to the sound of pouring rain and Gael barking as though something frightened her. She could hear the sheep bleating and Rán neighing and banging his hooves into the stall door. She sat up and grabbed her cane before standing. Surely, the storm wasn't scaring the animals this bad. She left her room, grabbed Gael by her collar, and pulled her back toward her room.

The dog instantly pulled free from Drea's grip and darted into the bedroom on her own. Once back in her room, unsure what was going on, Drea poked her head out of the room's doorway. At the end of the hallway, she could see a shadow about two and a half feet tall coming around the corner. She was frozen with fear. She couldn't look away. Just then, a thin, fury arm shaped like a half circle with long thin razor sharp claws at the end of it grabbed the wall. The rest of the creature rounded the corner and into the hallway.

It looked like a two foot tall shriveled up fig with arced appendages and long, deadly claws. She couldn't see its face. She slowly backed away from the doorway and hid behind the door to her room. Her heart thudded in her chest, fear and panic overwhelming her as clicking and guttural sounds headed her way.

She knew she had to do something! She waited until the creature reached the door, then she pushed the door she was hiding behind as hard as she could and hit the creature in the head. Disoriented, the creature shrieked and clawed at the door as she locked it. She could hear the claws beginning to tear up the door. Drea looked at Gael, the dog returned her gaze just before bounding up to the window and scratching at it desperately. Drea limped over to it, pushed it open and crawled out, Gael gladly following her. Drea hobbled to the barn door. She went faster as an unnerving click sounded somewhere behind her. Gael bolted ahead of her and pushed open the door with her paw and nose.

As she made it inside, the door was instantly shut behind her. She gasped as a hand slipped over her mouth and she was pulled into Ran's stall. Lukas gently shoved her into Khan's outstretched arms. Drea opened her mouth to speak but shut it as the clicking and guttural grunts sounded directly outside from where they hid. She closed her eyes, trying to stop a tear from falling. But it didn't help. The unwanted tear slid down her cheek anyway. Fear engulfed her heart like a wave covering a small rock on the shore. The creature began to work and claw its way through the wood on the outside walls of the barn. Lukas took hold of Drea's waist and slowly lifted her up onto Rán's back. Then Khan slid up behind her and took hold of Gael as Lukas tossed her up to him. Lukas moved away a blanket hidden beneath a pile of hay and pulled up a few slats of wood on the floorboard. He reached down and pulled out a large bow and a quiver full of sharp arrows. Drea stared at him, confused, as he headed toward another stall and opened it. Her jaw dropped when a giant black horse emerged with a weathered brown leather saddle already cinched up on its girth.

This horse was at least two hands taller than Rán and twice as muscular. Lukas swiftly turned back to Rán, slid the bridle over his head and handed the reins back to Drea. Rán plodded out of the stall and waited at the large barn door.

Lukas came up beside the horse's ear and whispered something. Drea didn't catch what he had said. She was amazed at Lukas who hoisted himself up onto the noble steed in one fluid motion, took an arrow from his quiver, nocked it and aimed at a thin piece of rope. As the arrow was released, she flinched and felt Rán tense. Just before the arrow hit its mark, both horses lunged forward. Drea's legs squeezed Rán's sides, and her hands held tight to the reins as the horse bolted out of the barn and onto a trail. The two horses raced down the path being chased by the dark creatures. She could hear the eerie shrieking clicks behind them. Drea gasped as she noticed several scars along the black horse's neck and haunches. *Has something like this happened before?* She wondered. Lukas turned in his saddle and nocked another arrow. She heard him click his teeth and his horse swiftly spun around on its haunches like a roping horse would and headed back the way they had come.

"Keep going!" Drea heard Lukas yell as he faded off into the distance back toward the farm.

"Don't look back," Khan said, pushing her face back to the trail ahead.

They galloped at top speed for about fifteen minutes and then Khan reined Rán in and slowed him to a trot then down to a walk. The horse had foam dripping from the sides of its mouth around its snaffle bit. Rán's sides were heaving with labored breaths from the extended run, but the twins could feel beneath them that this horse had more in him.

Thankful that they had gotten away from whatever that was, they found a safe spot and dismounted.

❄❄❄

Khan watched as Drea stroked Gael's and Rán's necks. Both animals had laid down beside her. While she stared into the campfire that Khan had built, Drea gasped. Khan instantly stood and looked around. Nothing seemed to be wrong. She looked at him sadly.

"We forgot Ariela." She whispered and hung her head. Khan sighed dismally. Ariela had always been Drea's home when things would go wrong, like when Khan was arrested because the gang he was a part of abandoned him just as officers came to take them. He had been cut off from the world in a small jail cell. Luckily, the officers discovered that Khan had never been involved in any of the scandalous things his gang did. Once he was released, Khan returned to find Drea literally sick from worry. Khan shook away these thoughts and sat down against Rán's broad back.

It had been at least an hour or two since they had gotten away to a safe spot. Rán had taken them to a small, enclosed area. Though Lukas was on his own, Khan figured that he could fend for himself. Khan stood as footsteps sounded around the bend of the trail just past the trees. Rán lifted his head and at the same time Gael flattened her ears and growled, both on high alert.

Lukas walked into the area, pulling his steed's reins. His left shoulder was bleeding, and he now walked with a limp. Khan heard Drea gasp and run toward him. She couldn't believe it! There was a white bundle of fluff curled up in Lukas's arms. Khan couldn't help but laugh. Drea was more concerned about Ariela than the person who had saved her. Lukas watched as Drea walked away, cuddling the scared cat in her arms. He walked over to where Khan stood and handed him the reins to his horse without a word then headed off into the dense brush surrounding their hideout. Khan studied the horse. It stared at him with bright eyes. Its mane slowly ruffled as a small wind blew through the area. Sadness crept into his heart as he saw how many scars marred the horse's flesh.

"What's its name?" Asked Khan, not looking away from the horse. "Koa the Radiant." Said Lukas proudly.

Khan looked back at him, entirely confused about what Lukas had said.

"What?" Asked Khan, his voice thick with an accent he had never really noticed until now.

Lukas laughed as he pushed down a branch that lifted a bed of leaves. A big tub of water lay underneath it. The horses neighed in delight and trotted over to it to drink. Lukas wiped his hands on a piece of cloth. After he was done, he put it in his back pocket. Khan could see initials on it. He glared at it, trying to see what they were.

"C and A." Drea's voice whispered in his ear, making him jump. Khan opened his mouth to ask how she knew what he was looking for and realized his twin normally knew what he was thinking, somehow.

"Her name is Koa the Radiant." Lukas's voice drifted into Khan's ears, bringing him back to the question at hand.

"What's 'the Radiant' for?"

"Well, Koa was a horse from the Onryx Kingdom. I got her when she was a foal. Horses from the Onryx Kingdom are usually considered gems. They are the fastest, strongest, and all are very beautiful and majestic. Throughout the kingdom, she was considered the most noble, brilliant, and radiant. Hence the name, Radiant." Lukas said with a wink.

"The High Lady, Aria, wanted Koa as her horse, but alas, she was already mine. During one of my travels, I found a white stallion, much like Koa, and I took him back to the Lady. She was most grateful. His name was Võr the Victorious."

Drea stared at Lukas, begging with her eyes to tell them more about the outer realms. There had been no one to tell them stories about the outer realms of the world. Lukas smiled as Khan sat down beside Drea, crossed his legs, held his head up with his hand and watched Lukas with half shut eyes. Lukas looked down at the pair of them and cleared his throat before proceeding with another story. Lukas would often pause during his stories to clean his shoulder wound with his handkerchief.

❄❄❄

After a much needed rest, and once Lukas felt it was safe, the three of them collected their things and, of course, the animals and headed back to Lukas's cabin.

Drea cautiously peered into the cabin, through a large space between the boards. The couch was on its side and torn open; almost everything inside was broken. She was dreading asking Lukas about those creatures that had chased them earlier. But Khan must have read her mind at that moment and posed the dreaded question.

"Some say they are called 'Bannons', dark creatures without scales or wings. I have tried to come up with an answer but the most logical thing would be necromancy. These creatures come once every month to pillage houses and scare the townsfolk. I've noticed that they even take a few things." Lukas said as he swept up the broken glass with an old broom.

Drea could only guess what necromancy was, she had never heard that word before. Whatever these creatures were, Lukas seemed to have a pure hatred for them. She looked back at Lukas as he cleared his throat, took something off the ground, folded it, and put it in his pocket. Drea walked past him and toward her room. As she touched the door handle, Lukas took hold of her shoulder.

"Uh, would you go and take care of Rán and Koa?" Khan moved to go with her to help, but stopped when Lukas said,

"No, Khan, you stay here and help me."

Drea sighed as she limped down the steps, took hold of Koa's and Rán's reins, and led them to the barn.

"Oh, Drea! Put Rán in a different stall!" Drea turned and nodded as she saw Lukas hanging out the door.

Drea pushed open the barn door. She had left the two horses outside and lit a few candles so she could see. As she turned back to the door to bring the horses in, a small creature fell from the ceiling and landed on top of her. The weight of it caused her to fall. She screamed at the top of her lungs, hoping Lukas and Khan would hear as she tried to keep the creature from her face. She shrieked as a foot sent it rocketing away from her. Khan immediately helped her up and pulled her out of the barn. Lukas stalked toward the creature and cornered it. Drea covered her ears and closed her eyes as the creature's shrieking click was cut off and ended in a guttural growl. Khan pulled her inside and shut the door.

Chapter III

The Wooden Boat

Light sparkled on the modest lake just beyond the pasture on Lukas's property. The morning was fresh and the air was crisp. Khan and Lukas had decided to go fishing. The two sat in a small wooden boat in the middle of the lake with fishing rods in their hands. Khan looked back at the shore and waved at Drea who was trying to get Koa and Rán to play with her. Each time she'd get close, they'd scatter. Every now and then, Gael would join in, careful not to get trampled. Khan's attention was drawn back to his fishing pole as it dived down toward the water. He panicked and stood up.

"Uh, uh, Lukas?"

"No! Khan, sit back down! You'll til---" Lukas wasn't able to finish his sentence as he and Khan fell over the sides of the boat.

Seconds later, Khan burst through the water's surface, gasping as he swam back to the boat. Lukas came up a second after him. His face was a mix of anger and laughter. Khan looked at him apologetically while Lukas pulled himself into the boat.

"Lukas! Khan!" Shouted a worried voice from shore. Khan and Lukas quickly looked at where Drea's voice came from. He gasped as he saw her hop onto Rán's back and watched helplessly as she darted away into the trees until he could no longer see her.

"Get down!" Hissed Lukas, shoving Khan down into the floor of the boat.

Khan stayed there for a while, waiting patiently for Lukas to give the word that it was safe.

"Hi, can I help you?" Said Lukas.

"Yes, sir. We are looking for two fugitives of the King. We had them, but they escaped. They've caused a lot of trouble in town. If you see them, it might be best if you let us know." Said a voice roughly.

Lukas gazed at Khan, his eyes full of questions. Khan met his gaze and shook his head.

"Right then, thanks for the warning. Now, be on your way and stop disturbing my stock." Lukas ordered. Khan grinned as he heard the guards give a dismissive grunt and a few choice words. He could hear the sound of the guard's horses retreating and fade off into the distance. Lukas let the boat drift toward the shore.

"Okay, you can come out now." Said Lukas.

Khan sat up and jumped out of the boat as soon as it touched land. He followed Rán's hoof prints to some trees behind the barn and found Drea holding tight to Rán's neck. Khan sighed with relief and touched Rán on the shoulder to get him to follow. The horse snorted and shook his head before following. Khan felt thankful and relieved when he walked out from behind the barn with his sister. But he also knew that this was a close call. Soldiers were searching for them. Khan didn't know why they were so important to the King. He knew one thing was for sure, that they wouldn't be able to stay here much longer.

"Khan, can you help me get off?" Asked Drea, her voice anxious. He nodded and put his palm on Rán's shoulder to make him stop. He took hold of Drea's waist, she leaned against his arms and he lifted her off. Khan grunted as he took her full weight and gently set her on the ground. He watched Drea lead Koa and Rán inside the barn before walking back to where Lukas stood.

"I don't think you both are safe here anymore." Said Lukas looking back toward the barn and at Drea.

"Why are they after us? We never burned down that shop. It was the King's soldiers. They were the ones that burned down our home. Even though it wasn't much of a home, we found refuge there. We didn't even once question or go against the King. Why would he care about two orphans who own nothing?" Exclaimed Khan as he followed Lukas inside the cabin.

Khan sighed as Lukas shrugged and walked to his room. Questions filled Khan's mind as he sat down on his bed. If he and Drea were a threat, why burn down their home instead of sending soldiers to peacefully extract them. Khan shivered and pushed the thought from his mind, then stood up and walked out of the cabin.

❄❄❄

Back at the barn, Drea softly swiped a medium-sized brush across Rán's back. The softness of his coat made her smile. He had the most beautiful and shiny brown coat she had ever seen. She didn't know what it was about this horse, but she definitely had a special bond with him.

She was pulled from her thoughts as Khan entered the barn and stood beside her. Drea turned toward him. He looked concerned and anxious. She drew a deep breath to ask what was wrong, but was cut off as Khan beat her to it.

"Drea, we have to leave. We can't stay here. We never could have." Said Khan, despair in his voice.

Drea gasped and took a step back as if Khan had struck her. Then she watched Khan turn away from her and with slumped shoulders, leave the barn. Her happy thoughts were stifled as she finished brushing Rán's coat and moved on to brush Koa down. She groaned when she heard Lukas calling for her to come back inside.

"Sorry, Koa. I'll finish up tomorrow." Said Drea. She walked out of Koa's stall, and closed the heavy wood door behind her. Koa snorted and stuck her head into the bucket hanging on the door of the stall where Drea had just dumped her grain. Drea slid her hands into her jacket pockets and she slowly walked back to the house. The sun was descending into the lake, shimmering across its surface as it sank. She stopped for a minute to take it in.

Drea breathed in sharply. Her chest felt like it was caving in, causing her vision to go black. An image flickered in her head. *She could see a vast desert and a volcano spewing lava. There was an image she couldn't quite make out. On the horizon, a creature trudged through the desert, as if searching for its home.*

Just before darkness enclosed her, *the image flipped and she saw the broad face of a dragon.* Then darkness...

❄❄❄

Khan soaked a damp cloth with cold water from the lake and dabbed Drea's forehead. He hated to see his sister like this, unable to control her seizures. This episode caused Khan to spend the whole night and half the next morning, worrying and taking care of her. Though Khan knew that it wasn't Drea's fault, he wished the seizure could have waited till morning. She had struggled to speak through the night, the seizure straining her vocal cords.

Footsteps sounded by the door, causing Khan to look back. "Go get some rest. I'll look after her now."

Khan nodded, stood up and walked out of their room and into the main room of the cabin. He trudged around the kitchen mindlessly.

He hadn't slept that night and hadn't eaten anything all morning. He tore off a handful of bread and bit into it. It was stale. He sighed and stepped out onto the front porch of the cabin and sat down on one of the steps.

He sat there for a bit, mindlessly chewing on the tough piece of bread. He was groggy for sure, and his thoughts were a bit jumbled up. He tried to clear his head as a voice muttered in his ear:

"The wings of war shall sound, As the fallen dragons make a song of sorrow and woe."

He tried to dismiss the voice in his head while he stared out at the lake. He jumped up as it sounded again. This time it was louder.

"The one in the water you must find, to truly be safe from the clutches of the Dragon Slayer."

Khan shook his head as he stumbled down the steps and jogged to the barn. Maybe going on a ride would clear his mind. *What did this mean?*

❄❄❄

Khan's agitation melted into calm as he relaxed into the saddle. He gazed down the fine trail, holding tightly to Rán's reins. The horse plodded purposefully down the trail. As he rode, Khan contemplated every reason as to why King Dolion was after him and Drea. The ride Khan took ended up in a blur, and he couldn't exactly remember why he had gone in the first place.

Once he was back at the barn, Khan put the horse in his stall but neglected to put away Rán's tack after he took it off. Khan walked out of the barn and toward the cabin as if he were in a daze. He stumbled inside and let out a long sigh as he collapsed on the couch and shut his eyes.

Chapter IV

The King's Soldiers

Khan, Lukas and Drea walked side by side down the road with their heads down so no one would recognize them. As they headed toward the town, they passed a squad of soldiers eating by a small fire. The men who had burnt down Drea's and Khan's home were King Dolion's soldiers. It was still fresh in their minds. And they were still looking for them. They needed to be careful.

They had waited to leave Lukas's home until Drea's ankle was healed enough for her to walk without help. Gael padded beside Drea, ready to help support Drea, if needed.

A small, stubby piece of wood spelled out the name of the street: Glenchaster. This was the busiest road she had been on in a while. She held her breath as carriages pulled by large white and black horses strolled by. The beauty of the graceful horses was breathtaking. She'd never seen anything quite like this before. There was so much to see, but little time to take it all in. Beautiful blossoming trees and townspeople everywhere.

A melancholy thought invaded Drea's mind wishing Ariela, her cat, had been able to see this. Lukas said they had to leave her, no matter how much Drea had begged to take her.

Lively conversations echoed around every corner. Several small shops and taverns were almost hidden in the trees. The vendors were busy striking up conversations with every passerby. This place was nothing like Orinshire. It was a fine-looking town, more lively than

Orinshire. The street itself was paved with red bricks in a diagonal pattern.

"This is closer to the kingdom. Things here are going to be finer than Orinshire or any of the outlying towns." Explained Lukas, his voice muffled by the cloth covering most of his face. Drea nodded, looking back to the street. Things were definitely nicer here.

❄❄❄

A short time later, they arrived at a luxurious inn. Drea limped up beside Lukas. Her jaw dropped. It was the largest inn she'd ever seen. The outside of the inn was a beautiful royal blue, and it boasted long golden pillars in the front that held up the balcony. Colorful flowers and foliage hung in baskets from the ceiling. "Are we even able to afford a room here?" Asked Drea breathlessly. Lukas let out a small chuckle and looked back at them.

"Oh. Of course we can!" Assured Lukas proudly.

Khan followed hesitantly behind Lukas as he jogged up the steps. He didn't exactly like the thought of sleeping in a fancy inn when people were obviously looking for them. He pushed the thought aside and ran after them. The inside was even prettier than the outside, if that were even possible! The ceiling in the common room had to be some thirty feet high, and the furnishings were lavish and well placed. Khan had never seen a place so big and grand.

Suddenly, Lukas walked past Khan and out the front door of the inn. Leaving Khan and Drea dumbfounded. They both looked at each other before Drea went out after him. Khan turned back to the concierge. A large man stood beside the booth, his arms crossed and his face covered. Khan gulped and trudged out of the inn.

"Hey! Wait! Who was that in there?" Questioned Khan as he took hold of Lukas's arm.

Lukas looked back, pulling away his arm from Khan's grip. He put a finger to his lips as his eyes flickered back to the inn. Khan glanced back to see the large man leaning against one of the golden pillars of the inn. Lukas pulled Khan and Drea away and down the street to a small vendor. There stood a lady whose hair was as white as snow. She glanced up and waved Lukas away with a shaking hand. Lukas said something to her in a language Khan had never heard before. She looked at him, her eyes full of fascination. She pointed a boney finger toward a small tavern across the street.

Lukas nodded his head and muttered something to her, then gently shook her hand before heading in the direction the old woman had told them to go. Lukas beckoned Drea and Khan to follow him. They both sighed and walked slowly after him toward the small tavern.

The trio crossed the street to the tavern, and every face turned toward them as they walked up the steps and into the pub. Once inside, it was dark and smoke-filled. The few people that were in the room stared at them as they walked past the tables.

Khan's eyes were drawn to two small paper posters nailed to the wall next to the cash register on the counter. One had Drea's face, the other Khan's. Both said **'WANTED, DEAD OR ALIVE.'** Lukas pushed past the people, took hold of Khan's and Drea's wrists and pulled them through the dimly lit eating area and up the stairs.

"Get in!" Lukas ordered as he shoved open a door and pushed them in.

Khan obeyed and stealthily slid into the room. Drea followed him inside with Gael by her side. Lukas came last and shut the door behind him. He sighed, his back to them. He slowly walked over to an unlit candle on a desk in the corner. Lukas took a match from a matchbox that was in his pocket, struck it on the side of the box and lit the candle before blowing out the match's flame. It illuminated the small room well enough. Drea plopped down on a broken couch, and called Gael over to her. The loyal dog put its head in her lap and she began to stroke it.

"Why were there two posters with our faces on them, Lukas? And who was that man? Why was he following us?" Khan pressed.

Lukas looked at him and opened his mouth to explain. He started to reply, but was cut off by several loud knocks at the door. Khan swiftly ran over to Drea and took hold of her, ready to run if needed. Lukas looked at them as he put his hand on the doorknob. Lukas motioned for them to hide. Khan and Drea dropped to the floor and hid behind the one bed as the door slowly creaked open.

"Hi there, dear. I was told to bring you some food. You didn't stay to get some." Said a high-pitched, annoying voice from the other side of the door. "Thank you." Said Lukas.

"Now, I'll just put this in and be on my merry way." The voice said.

"No need, I'll take it, love." Lukas insisted.

"No, no. I was told to personally deliver it into the room and check that the room is to your satisfaction." The voice argued. Khan jerked as a rough hand covered his mouth and pulled him up silently. Out of the corner of his eye, he could see the large man from the inn holding tightly to Drea, who was fighting as if it were her last day. The woman who was talking to Lukas screamed and left the room running. Gael let out a bark, but it was swiftly silenced as another man took hold of her and dragged her out the window.

Lukas gasped in horror, finally realizing what was happening. Khan let out a muffled scream, trying to warn Lukas as he drew his sword out of his pack and held it high. Khan heard a terrible sound then watched helplessly as Lukas slowly fell forward, landing roughly on the wooden floor.

❄❄❄

When Drea woke from her troubled sleep, she groaned and propped herself in a sitting position. She let out a grunt as her head hit wood. Drea seemed to be in a crate of some kind. She glanced around, darkness was all around her.

"Hello? Is anyone there?" She asked, her voice shaking.

An almost inaudible shuffle sounded by her feet.

"Khan?"

Drea jumped as Gael's face came into view in front of her.

"Hey, girl." Said Drea as her trembling hands reached for the dog's soft muzzle. She brought up her knees to her chest and rocked back and forth.

Drea let out a few giggles as Gael licked her face. Gael gently weaved around Drea's knees and tried to lay halfway in her lap. Stifling a sob, tears welled up in her eyes when she finally realized she was alone again.

❄❄❄

Someone pulled the wool cloth away from Khan's face making him squint at the bright light. The first thing to become visible was a large throne. A lean but tall man sat upon it with a modest, silver crown on his head. Lukas breathed heavily beside him as his gag was finally removed. Khan looked past Lukas, searching. Drea was nowhere to be seen, neither was Gael. Khan looked to his right, they were not there either. Anxiety turned into fear. Where was a Drea? Who had taken

PART II
THE ONRYX KINGDOM

Chapter I

Frode Jerrik

Sixteen years earlier

"Stay focused, Frode. We have to be precise. We can't afford any mishaps, *or* getting caught." Said Frode's brother, Jackson. Frode Jerrik and his brother's men headed toward the palace where the Great King Raconas Faelor and the Queen, Kaelera Faelor, resided. Frode nodded to his brother before following him down the slope and toward the palace. Here is where they would split up. They had talked through the plan many times. Four of the men would go in through the palace entrance where the merchants would come and go. It would be easier to blend in that way. But Frode and Jackson, his brother, would take a more direct route.

Frode Jerrik's heart pounded as he slid into the broken window after Jackson. His hand rested nervously on the hilt of his sword. After entering the palace hallway, Jackson put his fist in the air to motion for him to stop as steps sounded up the hall. A young maid came out of the shadows, she carried a bundle of cloth in her arms.

The maid looked up a second too late. Jackson's hand covered her mouth with a white cloth that held a deadly poison. He caught her just before she fell to the ground.

"Sorry, little lady." Said Jackson. Frode walked over to her, but turned away as she took her final breath. Together, they dragged her over to the wall and hid her behind heavy crimson brocade curtains. He quickly followed Jackson up a staircase and into the upper level of the palace. The whole way there, they encountered servants and guards whom they took care of in a swift but clean manner. In a few minutes, they met up with the rest of his brother's men.

"Emile, you take Howzer, Doyle, and Ilias. Go 'round back and take care of anyone who gets in your way. Me and Frode have this section of the palace covered." Said Jackson from behind Frode. He turned and watched his brother bid farewell to Emile.

"Come on, let's get moving." Whispered Jackson while he blew past Frode and ahead into the long corridor.

❄❄❄

Within minutes, Frode and Jackson had made it up to the King's sitting room and met up with the rest of their men. Before they entered the King's chambers, they discussed the best way to get in and out without getting caught.

Frode held tightly to his sword making his knuckles turn white. Emile, one of the men, began the silent countdown with his fingers. *Three, two, one.* Jackson stormed through the door first, his sword held high, but the King was ready for him. Several guards were poised and ready to fight. The Queen let out a shrill cry as Emile went after her. Frode battled intensely with one of the guards. Out of the corner of his eye, he could see that only he, Jackson, and Emile were left to stand against the King and his guards.

"Regroup!" Ordered Jackson.

Emile and Frode instantly fell back to Jackson with their swords poised and ready. The King and his remaining guards stood like a barrier to protect the Queen. Through the cracks, Frode noticed that the Queen stood in front of a cradle.

The young maid that stood beside the Queen reached into the cradle and pulled something out. The King noticed Frode's attention on the Queen and the cradle and lunged toward him. Frode parried and successfully blocked the blow. As the King focused on Frode, the remaining guards went after Emile and Jackson.

Frode grabbed the hilt of the King's sword as it came too close and pulled the King closer to him. Before the King thrust his shoulder into him, Frode was able to drive his jagged knife into the King's leg.

The King roared and side-swiped Frode with his foot, sending him to the floor. As Frode crawled away, the King pulled out the knife and held it tightly in his right hand, with his sword in his left. Frode looked behind the King

and saw Emile charging toward the Queen, who was whispering to the young maid. Jackson was nowhere to be seen.

Frode's heart pounded as he backed into the wall. The King pressed in on him. Out of nowhere, Jackson launched himself onto the King's back, driving his knives into his shoulders. The King howled and groaned as Jackson's weight pulled him backward and down to the floor. Frode glanced toward the Queen and saw the maid escaping through a side door of the chamber with a bundle of cloth in her arms. Emile had the Queen up against the wall, but she had one of the guards' swords in her hand that kept Emile at bay.

Frode's attention turned back to the King, who rose to his knees and tore out the knives. Jackson also stood up. "Go after her!" Ordered Jackson as the maid disappeared from the room.

Frode nodded and chased after her. Behind him, the King let out a furious cry. The King gained on him and drove his blade into Frode's left shoulder. He fell to the ground and turned back to see the King standing in front of him.

Just then, the King's eyes went blank as the hilt of a sword hit the back of his head. The giant man fell to his knees before collapsing face-first in front of Frode. The Queen screamed defiantly and broke away from Emile to protect her husband. She gasped as Emile's sword swiped across her left leg. She fell to the floor and crawled backward to where her husband lay, and away from the point of Emile's sword. Her teary eyes met Frode's as she glanced up from holding her husband's face in her hands. Emile and Jackson surrounded them, their swords at the ready in case she tried anything.

"Go, Frode." Said Jackson wearily.

Frode stood and ran unsteadily in the direction the maid went. After navigating his way through the palace, Frode made it out into the gardens, then into the forest. After a few minutes, he could see the maid carefully making her way through the forest up ahead of him on an obscure path. Frode tracked her quietly, waited for the right moment then launched himself at the maid. He dove at her, grabbed her legs and caused the young girl to fall to the ground. As she fell, she lost the grip on the bundle of cloth she was holding and it tumbled away from her. She tried her hardest to make it a soft landing for the delicate package she had been entrusted with.

Frode stood and walked around her pressing his blade to her throat. She looked to be barely seventeen winters old. He shook away the sentiment. As he was about to thrust his blade into the girl's chest, a pitiful cry erupted from the bundle of cloth. Frode glanced at the bundle, confused as the girl gasped when he walked over to it. *What was so special about a bundle of cloth?* Frode wondered.

His heart jumped when he pulled the cloth away to reveal the faces of two small infants. They seemed to be only a few weeks old. He looked back at the young maid.

"Please. They are just new-borns." Cried the girl as tears slowly rolled down her cheek.

Frode backed away. He didn't sign up to slaughter innocent children, babies at that. The girl stared at him fearfully as he gestured toward the bundle with his sword.

"Go." He said. "Say nothing and go. Don't ever come back."

The girl quickly scrambled over to the bundle that lay on the ground and grabbed the infants with trembling hands.

"Thank you." The young maid said before Frode turned away. Not waiting for the maid to leave, he shook his head and ran back toward the palace.

As Frode came up to the palace's door, Emile came out and patted him on the shoulder before leading him into the throne room. The King was on his knees beside the Queen, who was shaking violently. A man, maybe the King's age or a little younger, stood staring at them with his face covered. Jackson stood beside the man, but turned to greet Frode who had just come back from chasing the maid. "Did you get her?" Asked Jackson. Frode's breath caught in his throat, he wasn't the best at lying. "Yes." He answered dryly.

His brother nodded, patted his shoulder before he walked away, leaving him and the man staring at the King and Queen.

"The Country of Sonerian thanks you." Said the man before he walked away. Frode tried to catch a glimpse of the man, but his face was covered. The Queen looked up, finally noticing him, and let out a sigh of remorse then laid her head on the King's shoulder. The King glared at Frode with anger and defeat in his eyes. Emile grabbed Frode's shoulder and pulled him away after Jackson.

❄❄❄

Drea

Present Day

Drea numbly walked beside Malcolm, a man who led the soldiers of Wolfed. She held tight to Gael's leash as they passed several street people begging for money or food. Drea couldn't help but feel sorry for the peasants as she walked by. She understood their needs all too well.

Three months ago, Drea woke up to Malcolm and two young boys peering into her crate. Fearful and anxious, Drea sat there frozen as they questioned her. When she asked where she was, they simply answered,

"The Great King Dolion so graciously gifted you to us, my dear."

In these past three months, Drea had been forced to train to fight, and was forced to stay at this rudimentary camp. They, surprisingly, let her keep Gael. She was good at fighting, and in a way enjoyed it. She sighed as she shut her eyes and tried to push away the thoughts of the past few months. Her dirty black hair was pulled back into a tight braid. While she crossed a puddle, she snuck a glance at her face, it looked harsh. She barely recognized herself. Malcolm was briefing Drea on her next assignment, which was also her last one before she could become a true assassin. She shivered as she felt the cold, brisk fall wind ripple through her clothes. It felt as if the wind disliked the idea. She agreed. She didn't like it either.

This would be the seventeenth fall Drea had seen. It would also be the seventeenth for her twin brother, Khan. Drea shook away the thought as sadness began to burn through the cold. Would she ever see him again? Will she live long enough to perhaps track him down?

"What is my assignment?" Asked Drea as she followed Malcolm up the hill.

"All in good time, my dear. All in good time."

❄❄❄

Drea slipped unnoticed through the waves of people in town shortly after receiving her mission orders. Her rawhide coat hid her weapons from any passerby. Gael followed closely to her. They entered a local tavern and stepped up to the counter.

The man Drea was targeting was the man who supposedly put an end to the previous Great King Raconas reign. This man was of high value to King Dolion. Drea was more afraid of him than anything, considering he wanted her and Khan dead. Malcolm had told her that King Dolion would go to great lengths to hunt down his enemies and those who would defy him.

Drea's anxiety was higher than normal this time. This was not like her other missions, no, it was much worse. She was expected to ki— (she hated to think about it), or to take someone out. That sounded like a much nicer way to put it.

She considered running, but Malcolm had the best trackers in the kingdom. She had found this out the hard way. She had tried to escape them more than once. They'd be able to find her wherever she went.

She laid her elbows on the counter and beckoned the server. She was an older woman with graying hair and a tired looking posture.

"How can I help you, hon?" She asked, weariness clinging tightly to her words.

"I'm looking for Frode Jerrik." Drea whispered into the woman's ear.

The lady sucked air through her teeth before taking a piece of crumpled parchment out of her pocket and a charcoal pencil out of her hair. She quickly scribbled something down, folded the parchment over, handed it to Drea and briskly walked away. It said,

He will meet you outside.

At your own risk, young'un.

Drea read the message quickly before she crumbled it up in her hands, and dropped it on the floor.

Once outside the tavern, Drea stopped abruptly when she heard Gael let out a whine that was quickly cut off. She turned around to see Gael, her dog being held to the ground.

There was a short, well-upholstered man struggling on the ground with his knee pressing on the dog's neck. His meaty hand gripped her muzzle shut. Another man, taller but lithe, came out of the shadows.

"I hear you've been looking for me, eh?" The man said, showing his dingy, yellow teeth. "Word travels fast," Drea said to him. Slowly, Drea lifted her hand up into her coat and grabbed the hilt of a small, thin sword. Jerrik noticed and shook his finger at her. "Ah, ah. Try anything and I'll put a slug in your dog's chest. I'm guessing you don't want that to happen, do ya?"

Drea bit her lip. She let out an agitated sigh and let her hand drop, but she kept her other hand close to the dagger that was concealed beneath her belt. Now, she would feel better if she had to hurt someone for threatening her dog. "So, you're a part of the fanatic group that calls themselves 'High Servants of the King.' Do you know the reason you are after me today?" Grumbled Frode while he studied his nails.

"That's funny, I figured you to be the *fanatic* here." Said Drea while she straightened her posture.

Her ears burned as she heard the slow creeping of someone coming up behind her. Drea twisted and grabbed the prowler's hair and tugged them in front of her, with her knife at their throat.

It was a young boy, a few years younger than her. Fear and shock spread across Jerrik's face. "Let's make a trade, eh, Jerrik?" Drea said, allowing herself to grin madly. Clearly this boy meant something to him. She was good at exploiting weakness.

Jerrik looked at Gael and then back at the boy. Drea thought she saw tears in Jerrik's eyes. The man holding Gael gaped at him.

"Let the stupid dog go, now!" Hissed Jerrik at his henchman. Drea waited until Gael was by her side before shoving the boy forward. The force caused him to stumble and fall at Jerrik's feet. As Drea swiftly drew her sword, Jerrik swung out a small pistol. She heard a loud bang and then felt a burning sensation as the bullet hit her right shoulder. In pain, she turned and ran as fast as she could. She heard Jerrik and his men yell as they chased her down the street. She gritted her teeth, trying not to panic. Her shoulder throbbed and blood slowly spilled into her hand.

A shadow followed her from above. Drea skidded to a halt as she rounded a corner, and pulled her hood over her head. Hoping she would lose them, she pressed her way through and melted into a crowd of people. Gael led Drea through the holes in the crowd and eventually ended up near a ruin just outside the town. It looked like she had gotten away from Jerrik and his men. She stumbled up the steps and sat against the dilapidated sandstone wall. Drea drew her knife, cut off a strip of her shirt and tied it around the wound on her shoulder. She took one side of the strip of cloth in her teeth and the other in her hand and pulled as tight as she could. She groaned in pain, but swiftly silenced herself as voices came from the bottom of the ruins.

A pistol was the second most lethal of weapons available, and very hard to acquire. Only the most powerful people in the kingdoms owned one. Typically, only the King's soldiers had this kind of weapon.

Drea stood and peered out of the shadows where she sat. Thinking it was safe, she started back down the steps, and stepped out into the sun. A set of hands covered her mouth and grabbed her

waist. She kicked and screamed as she was pulled away into the shadows.

"Shut up!" A familiar sounding voice urgently whispered in her ear.

Drea instantly stopped struggling and obeyed the voice as Jerrik and his men ran this way and that, arguing about which way Drea had gone.

She sighed in relief as she recognized Jax. She pushed away his hand but realized Gael was not around.

"Wait. Where's Gael?" Drea asked, glancing around. Jax shook his head.

"I'm not sure." He said before he walked away.

❃❃❃

Jax and Drea decided to split up to see if they could find any trace of Gael.

With Jax choosing to go to the east side of the ruins, Drea headed to the west side. Once she came around the front of the buildings, she caught sight of three men dragging something through the dirt. Fury invaded her thoughts as she ran in that direction. Heart pounding, she held her sword firm in one hand and flung her small jackknife that was in her other hand at the closest man's back. He let out a cry of pain and fell to the ground. The thrill of the chase always got to Drea.

Now, there was a different element. Anger. Thrill turned to rage when she saw Gael bloodied and being dragged through the dirt. She roared and jumped just before she got to the men and swung both her sword and dagger across their backs.

They both bellowed in pain and dropped their hold of Gael. Drea shoved the men away from Gael, pulled the dog up to her chest and took off.

❄❄❄

"Drea. You have failed your mission." Malcolm stated firmly. Drea shuddered, but thought she heard a morbid satisfaction rising in his voice. Drea looked away from where he stood, pain and sadness overwhelming her. She had killed one man and brutally injured two others. Everyone seemed to think it was a good thing, but she had still failed.

Drea felt ashamed, as though she'd never be considered good or gentle again. Blood now forever stained her hands. This was the first time she had killed someone. While she battled with her thoughts, she heard everyone gasp as the doors of their refuge were thrown open. Several of King Dolion's soldiers poured in and surrounded her. She looked up as the soldiers parted to let a man through. Drea's breath caught her throat as King Dolion stood in front of her, his hands behind his back and a large golden crown on his head. "I need you to take care of someone for me, dear."

She felt numb, she was in pain, but there was another mission.

❄❄❄

Later, Drea had slowly made her way to the infirmary. She sighed in relief as Chalon finished stitching up her shoulder wound. Chalon was the medic in this society.

Chalon noticed Drea's anxiety when she prepared a linen sling for Drea's shoulder before continuing to work on Gael. "Don't worry, Gael will be okay with some rest. Though, I'm sure neither of you will get any of that anytime soon." Said Chalon, giving Drea a side glance.

Drea studied her. She wondered how long Chalon had been here and if she had been forced to stay like Drea had been. The woman's hair was starting to thin and turn gray. She wondered if Chalon ever regretted coming to this town. Gael whined as she met Drea's gaze.

"Chalon. I don't think I can go through with it." Whispered Drea.

Chalon gazed at her, her green eyes shining in the fire light. She shook her head and sat down on a small chair and looked at Drea. "Honey, be careful what you say and do. Alright? They've got eyes on you ever since you came to this awful place." Chalon said while she pulled off her gloves.

Drea nodded in thanks, took Gael in her arms and walked off. Gael whimpered and whined as Drea walked back to the common room. She stopped just before she entered the room, thought better of it and left to go back to her room. She kicked open her door, stepped in and closed it with her foot. She set Gael gently on her bed, walked over to her window and sat down. She was weary and her mind was troubled. Looking out of her window, she sighed as she thought about the 'mission' that King Dolion had given her. Something else bothered her about this. Dolion had come after her and Khan and tried to kill them, but now he wanted her to kill someone for him. It didn't make any sense. Why did the King choose her for the mission? A question she will forever ask herself! She hated to think about what she was now a part of. She didn't even harm a hair on Frode Jerrik's head, but she had killed one of his men. As she thought about these things, her door swung open and two of King Dolion's soldiers walked in.

"We're taking you to the castle, where you will be briefed and will collect your supplies." One of the soldiers announced as the other took Gael in his arms and walked out with Drea in tow.

Chapter II

The Golden Frame

Khan gently slowed his horse into a trot as he came upon the palace's gates. He had been out on patrol duty all night and had earned himself some well deserved rest. Slowing down further, his steed eased into a walk as the gates slowly opened. Khan reached down and patted her neck. A young stable boy came running up to him and took hold of the horse's reins and Khan slid off. He patted the boy on the head, nodding his head in thanks before strolling toward the castle doors. As Khan walked through the large halls, he was fascinated by the paintings on the wall. Each one showed a particular battle that Onryx had fought and won. Somehow, each painting elegantly depicted the struggle that led to the triumph.

Finally, back at his room, he opened his door and sighed. His room was bigger than what he was used to. Too big for his taste. Drawings were laid across his desk, one of them was encased in a golden frame. It was of Drea and Gael. They had sent numerous search parties, but each one came up empty, with no clues or leads to where Drea might be. A tear slowly slid down his cheek while he held it in his hands. Each night, it was all the same, the same feelings and the same thoughts. Even losing Gael took a toll on Khan's mood. He hadn't cared much for animals, but how much Drea loved Gael made an impact. Lord Ragnar had finally declared Drea to be lost to them. It had been three months of searching, there was nothing else they could do. Khan slowly put the frame down and walked over to his bed. He undressed and plopped down on his bed, exhausted.

He knew she was still alive; he could feel it. He would find her, somehow. He laid his head down, closed his eyes and began to drift into a restless sleep.

The next morning, Khan walked beside Lukas, his boots clicking against the hallway floor. The High Lord Ragnar followed them quietly. Khan was surprised to find out that Lukas and Ragnar were related. They certainly seemed to dislike one another. After Lord Ragnar had snatched Khan, Lukas and Drea, he claimed to have rescued them because Khan and Drea were "special". Khan didn't really believe anything Ragnar had said. None of it made any sense.

Things between Khan and Lukas had become bitter. Khan hated people keeping secrets from him. He felt as though he had been left in the dark about so many things. As Khan was lost in his thoughts, he didn't hear the person coming up behind him. He grunted as the person crashed into him in a panic.

"My Lord! Lord Ragnar!" The man said as soon as he recovered.

Khan shook his head and walked after him. The man was one of Ragnar's scribes. He was obviously concerned and needed to speak what he knew.

"Lady Helene has just sent word she is preparing to visit. She'll be here within less than a fortnight. Your Lordship." The scribe explained as he drew in a large breath.

"Oh! Well, we must be ready for her, yes?" Ragnar suggested. Khan watched Lord Ragnar walk away with a determined strut. He looked at Lukas, whose face was a mask of amusement, slapping the scribe on the back. Khan wondered how much Lukas actually worried about Drea or Gael. As Khan walked back to his room, he heard Lukas calling to him to wait.

Khan ignored his demands and slid into his room and locked the door. "Khan! Please. I'm sorry." Pleaded Lukas as he softly rapped on the door. Ignoring his pleas, Khan tore off his heavy lace jacket and layed it over the chair. He had nothing to say to this man. Lukas had betrayed Khan. He had trusted Lukas with his life. He had just found out that Lukas's search party gave up searching for Drea. That hurt Khan more than anything to know that this man, who was like a father to him, gave up on his only sister and the only family he had ever known. Another knock came at his door, tearing him from his thoughts.

"Go away, Lukas!" Khan shouted at the door and he walked over to his desk.

"Uh, Master Khan? Something is going on with Duma." Said a young voice outside the door. Khan quickly grabbed his coat and charged out the door, following after the stable boy. The boy was rushing and appeared anxious. Something had to be wrong.

❄❄❄

Khan's heart pounded as he entered the stables and headed toward Duma's stall. This was the horse he had been given by Lord Ragnar. He had developed a special bond with her. As Khan arrived at Duma's stall, he overheard the medic asking how much Duma had been eating.

His heart stopped as he saw Duma lying down on her side, her sides heaving in apparent pain. The medic stood up and turned toward Khan.

"This looks like colic. It's pretty bad. I can't get her to stand. I don't believe she will make it to the morning." He whispered in Khan's ear before walking out, the stable hand following behind him.

Khan walked over to Duma, sat down by her head and gently lifted it onto his lap. It broke his heart as he listened to her grunt and groan.

He laid his head back on the wall of Duma's stall and closed his eyes while he stroked her neck.

Khan couldn't remember the last time he had cared so much for an animal. For the past few months, Duma took care of Khan. She always took him down the safest paths. He drew in a shaky breath, brought his head to Duma's, and kissed her soft forehead.

"It'll be okay." He whispered.

❄❄❄

Khan woke with a start as he felt Duma's weight shift. He studied her for a moment. She grunted as she struggled to stand. Tears began to sting his eyes. Duma proved everyone wrong as she slowly stood up and shook the straw from her soft coat. Khan stood up with her and let out a laugh of joy. He swung his arms around her broad neck and laughed again as Duma bent her head around him and touched it gently to his back.

"Charles!" Khan called as he let go and took a step back. "She's okay!"

The stable boy stopped at the stall door and hung over it. His eyes were full of happiness and relief. Khan could finally understand what Drea felt for these animals. Duma nickered and gently tousled the boy's hair with her soft nose. He giggled, pulled away from the door, reached down and opened the stall door. He handed Khan a lead rope. Khan smiled when he saw Duma's name written at the top of it as he slid it over her head.

"Where shall we take her?" Asked Khan as he gazed at the boy.
"We? Milord?" Asked the boy, stunned.

Khan nodded and began to lead Duma out of the stall, hoping the boy would come with him.

"We could take 'er to the hilltop, milord."

Khan let out a laugh as the boy came bounding up to Duma's other side.

"Of course! What a marvelous idea." Agreed Khan before he led Duma out of her stall and into the open.

❄❄❄

After their walk to the nearby hilltop, Khan watched the stable boy slowly make his way back to the stables. It was time for him to saddle the horses for the patrol guards. Khan had declined the boy's offer to take Duma back with him, saying he wanted to walk Duma a little longer.

It was a beautiful place and the morning was fresh. The sea was visible outside the palace gates and he wanted to head back that way. Just as Khan turned his horse around, he saw something fly out of the water and into the clouds. Fear provoked Khan to grab Duma's lead and get her back to safety. He clicked his tongue and turned her around. As he led her down the stone walkway back toward the palace stables, Lukas came running up to meet him. Khan let out a sigh, trying to cover up his anger and distrust. Lukas caught up to him and walked on the other side of Duma.

"Khan, Lady Helene is coming sooner than expected. Now, Khan, she has, eh, different ways of travel. You'll understand what I mean when she arrives." Stated Lukas as Khan put Duma in her stall.

Khan nodded in acknowledgment and then walked away from him. Lukas groaned and followed after him.

"Khan, I know that I lied to you." Said Lukas. Khan wanted to forgive and believe Lukas, but something told him to be cautious. Khan stopped, turned toward Lukas and glared at him for a few moments. Lukas sighed, hung his head and said, "I'm sorry."

Silence fell between the two as they walked out of the stables and toward the palace. A few of Lord Ragnar's scribes hurried toward them with robes flailing. Lukas greeted them as they walked past, they nodded their heads in reply.

"You know, I never wanted to come back here. Ever since my wife died, this place carries too many sad memories." Said Lukas as they walked down the corridor.

Khan stared at him questioningly. He never knew that Lukas had a wife. Then again, Khan didn't seem to know anything about Lukas anymore. He scoffed to himself.

A small part of Khan felt sorry for the man, but he wasn't sure it was enough to forgive him. Since Drea was taken from him, it seemed like everything had turned gray for Khan. In his heart, Khan knew they had done all they could to get his sister back. As he arrived at his room, he couldn't help but feel grateful for all they have done for him. He was being treated well, and this was a beautiful and peaceful place in which to live. But he was reminded every day of his loss.

Chapter III

Sunrise Above Decks

Drea slid down from her hammock and headed up to the top deck of the ship. In many ways, the journey was enjoyable. However, the whirling sea made her a little seasick. As she gazed at the approaching dawn, she wished the morning would be delayed. It had been a rough week at sea, but today was the day everything would go down. Her mission was about to begin. She let out a slow sigh as she looked down at the water below.

She touched her shoulder that had been hit by Frode's bullet, it was aching again.

She wished for her old life back. She wished this wasn't happening, that she was back at home with Khan and Ariela before Lukas came into their life. Back when it was just the two of them and they were happy. She glanced up toward the pink morning sky. A bright, golden star seemed to settle right above her. This caused her to smile.

"Hi, Mom." Whispered Drea while she gazed at the fading star in the early morning sunrise.

Drea and Khan only had very few memories of their parents. The only thing Drea remembered about her father was his long, dirty blonde hair, and his pearly smile. Her mother, on the other hand, Drea remembered almost every feature. She had kind blue eyes and the most beautiful red hair that shimmered gold in the sunlight. Drea could almost remember her voice along with the lullabies she used to sing to her and Khan.

Drea's smile faded and she lost her train of thought when the sound of heavy feet sounded all around her. She glanced at an opening in the ship as several shouts and yells came out of it. Drea laughed and walked over to it. She met Gael on the stairs being held down.

"It's okay, I have permission to have her aboard."

"Yes, madam. We just thought…" The man started.

Drea stifled a laugh. Gael thrust her head up and cracked the man in the jaw. Drea apologized to the man when Gael bounded up the stairs and past her. The man nodded. There was anger and embarrassment in his eyes as he walked back down the stairs.

After all the excitement, Drea strolled back to her room with Gael at her side. She realized the Lady, to whom she was a servant, wasn't anywhere on the ship.

She scoffed to herself as she walked into her room that held nothing but a good-sized hammock and a trunk for necessities. She was assigned to be a servant to a self-absorbed Royal. King Dolion said it was less conspicuous if she entered the kingdom as a servant to the Lady herself. She sighed, Lady Helene didn't even know what would happen once the time came for Drea to complete her duty. King Dolion gifted Drea to serve Lady Helene, or so the Lady was told. King Dolion had to have people smuggle Drea's weapons onto the ship. This trip that Lady Helene was making was peaceful, and diplomatic. Only the Lady's guards were permitted to hold and carry weapons.

Drea gasped as one of the ship's captains bellowed that one phrase that Drea dreaded most to hear.

"Land ho!"

Drea swiftly put her servant's clothing on. She was a little disgusted by the color. A bright green and dingy brown frock was given to her to wear.

She was glad, however, for the black veil that covered her face. She stared at her hair. King Dolion had her hair dyed to match the servants of Lady Helene. It was a dull brown with an ugly green tint on the tips. Well, it was ugly to her anyway. She quickly put it up into a bun and pulled a few strands out to dangle outside the veil. Gael watched her, anxiety showing in her eyes. Drea sighed, she had to leave Gael on the boat until she had permission to bring her into the Kingdom.

"You'll be okay. It will all be over soon." Said Drea as she kissed Gael's soft head and walked out.

I hope. Drea added silently to herself. She followed the other servants to the tenders and climbed in. Drea kept silent as the first-mate rowed them to the docks where they were met by several guards. Each guard had a sword and a musket strapped to their side. She gulped as she took the hand of a soldier and climbed out of the boat. She tried to keep herself from breathing heavily. She could feel the cold gaze of the soldier on her. He led her to a large carriage and instructed her to get inside. The guard took hold of her hand once more to help her up the tall steps before walking back to collect the next servant.

Drea gaped at the approaching kingdom, it was the most beautiful thing she'd ever seen. She watched the people walk by as the four white horses pulled the large carriage through the streets amid the vendor markets and shops. Drea had never seen anything like it. Her jaw dropped as she caught a glimpse of the palace. It was almost the size of King Dolion's palace.

Drea left the carriage second and quickly followed behind Lady Helene's lady's maid. "Come, child." Said the servant.

Drea gulped and walked up to her side. She was the one who was training Drea in the ways of being a servant. This maid told her many things including that she thought that Lady Helene was a rude mistress. Though it seemed that the maid herself was the rude one.

"How will I handle that?" Drea had asked sarcastically under her breath, hoping the lady's maid didn't hear. They walked silently through the corridors and into the servant's quarters. The lady's maid taught Drea what each item for brushing the Lady's hair was called. She also told Drea to let Lady Helene choose the dress to wear. Everyone stopped in their tracks as loud shouts came from outside.

"She's here!" Clamored the servants as they quickly went out the back and made their way to the front of the palace.

Drea held her veil down with one hand as the wind blew fiercely at her, chilling her bones. Shock and amazement overtook her from the scene that lay in front of her. It took everything she had to not fall to the ground. A large, green dragon slowly glided to the front of the palace. The earth shuddered when the dragon landed. Her heart was beating out of her chest. Drea let her terrified eyes look over the dragon's unique features.

Leaves and small branches made up its flesh. Its tail was studded with rocks that stopped at its spine. Everything Drea believed in was proven wrong when the dragon let out an ear-splitting roar. She shuddered and covered her ears. She stared in disbelief as a lean figure slid down from the dragon's back and landed lightly on the stone. Drea couldn't believe this. It couldn't be real!

As she watched on, three tall and well dressed men walked out to greet Lady Helene. One of them was Lord Ragnar. Drea watched as Lady Helene whispered something to the dragon. Right after the dragon nodded, it looked directly at Drea. Her heart was in her throat as its eyes appeared to connect with hers. It roared once more, beat its powerful wings and launched itself upward into the sky.

❄❄❄

Drea's heart pounded in her chest as she walked behind Lady Helene. She could have sworn someone could hear her heartbeats. As

Drea followed the maids, she froze in her tracks. A familiar face came around the corner and walked past the servants, tipping his head to Lady Helene.

There he was, standing there, with his thick black hair and a long scar traveling from his chin to the collar of his shirt.

Chapter IV

Võr

"You must take Võr. Duma will only be your pleasure horse. She's not in any condition to see much action." Lukas had said before Lord Ragnar could say anything.

Khan glared at Lukas with wide eyes full of defiance. Khan stood his ground and pleaded his case regarding Duma. He argued that he would never have another horse.

"Just wait until you see him before you make up your mind." Stated Lukas.

Fine! Said Khan abruptly.

❄❄❄

Khan and Lukas made their way to the stables and over toward Võr's stall. The large white horse slowly clopped over to them and rested its nose in Lukas's hands. Võr pulled away and turned to Khan. He snorted and bobbed his head up and down.

"He was my wife's horse." Whispered Lukas as he tenderly touched his finger to the horse's nose.

"You said he belonged to the High Lady Aria." Stated Khan, furrowing his brow.

Realization hit Khan as Lukas looked at him, his eyes glistening with tears. Khan couldn't find the right words to ask: Did that mean Lukas had once been a Lord? Khan guessed he should have been able to put it together since Lukas's brother, Ragnar was Lord of the Onryx Kingdom. Lukas smiled, and wiped at his eyes before patting the stall door. Without another word, Lukas turned and walked over to Koa's stall.

Lord Ragnar sent a group of soldiers back with Lukas to his home. He had demanded to go back to collect his things along with his two horses, Koa and Rán. Much to Khan's relief, he had brought Ariela back too, Drea's little white cat. Khan smiled as he saw her walking along the stall doors.

She was a barn cat now. Khan slowly eased open the stall door, grabbed Võr's lead and pulled him out into the walkway. The horse's hooves clopped loudly on the stone as Khan led him to a larger area to put on his tack. All the while, Khan marveled at the muscular body that Võr had. He was perfectly fit and had been groomed well.

Charles, the young stable boy, watched from afar, his mouth hanging open while Khan walked Võr out of the stables.

Khan put his left foot into the stirrup and slowly eased himself into the saddle on Võr's broad back. Khan glanced to his left as Koa's familiar head came up beside him. Lukas sat a full head taller than Khan on Koa. Koa was almost one hand taller than Võr. Though Koa was taller and stronger, Võr seemed regal and agile.

"Keep up, old man." Taunted Khan as he squeezed his heels into Võr's sides.

Khan grunted as Võr reared, and leaped forward. Once his hooves touched the ground, it felt like Khan was flying. The cold air rushed through his lungs, and stung his eyes. He drew a deep breath to let out a whoop. Khan couldn't help but let out bursts of laughter as Lukas and Koa struggled to keep Võr's speed. The two horses continued at top speed thundering through the trail that led up toward the cliff. Time seemed to slow as Khan and Võr came up to the top of a cliff.

Võr reared when lightning struck right by his hooves. Khan let out a yelp and almost fell to the ground. He held on tightly to Võr's mane. When Võr's front hooves touched back onto the soggy earth, Khan leaned forward and patted Võr's neck and said,

"Easy. Easy, boy."

Võr flared his nostrils and snorted in fear. There must be something beyond the edge of the cliff or in the immediate area that seemed to have put the horse on edge, reasoned Khan. Lukas and Koa stood staring at the two. A soft rain had now begun to fall. As Võr trotted back, Khan twisted in the saddle and looked back at the cliff. He thought he saw a small creature climbing up the cliff. It was eerily similar to one of those creatures that came and wrecked Lukas's home. *Were they following them?* Wondered Khan while he urged Võr into a stable trot.

"Come on. Let's get back so we can get ready for the ceremony." Said Khan as he passed Lukas on his way back down.

❄❄❄

Later that day, Khan laid down on his bed, staring at the coral painted ceiling. He mulled over all that had happened that day. As Khan gazed at the ceiling, he saw something he'd never seen before. He sat up and started to really study the ceiling. There was a large, winged snake slithering through the reeds and coral of a deep pool of water painted on the ceiling. It blended in with the surrounding colors of green and blue. It was almost hidden and seemed unnatural. He took in a sharp breath as he met the serpent's eyes and a vision eclipsed his mind.

Khan was engulfed in water. He gasped and coughed as the salt water burned his throat. He was sinking further down and desperately tried to get back to the surface, but to no avail.

The water began to flood his lungs. After what seemed like several minutes of struggling for air, Khan gradually started to breathe. Hundreds of bubbles came from his mouth and nose as he breathed out. Relief overtook Khan as his breath came back to him. He could now see an unbelievable scene unfold in front of him. There was a series of caves hidden by dense coral colonies and reed beds.

Amazed at what he was seeing, Khan was startled as two dragons blew past him and headed down a steep slope. Khan tried to make sense of what he was seeing. He didn't know why, but he felt compelled to go down after them.

One was the color of a clear, early night sky, it reminded him of the color of twilight. The other was green and blue, like the color of the turquoise water in the South Seas. Khan slowed to a stop in front of a tall cave. He paused. Everything inside of him was telling him to go in. However, the darkness of the water made him wary. But he couldn't shake the feeling that something was hidden in there and he needed to find it. He backed up when he heard a loud roar come from the bottom of the canyon. Peering over the edge, he saw the blue dragon caught in a thick bed of sea kelp. Khan watched intently as the great blue dragon struggled to get untangled. He looked back to the cave behind him and decided to go inside. After a while of swimming through the chilly, dark water of the cave, he could see an embankment from below the water. When Khan finally surfaced, he crawled up onto the rocky embankment and was stunned at the scenery inside the cave. Gold and green algae glistened on the sides of the cave and hung from its ceiling.

In the middle of the cave lay a small white and gold egg.

As Khan reached out to touch it, he was pulled away by some unseen force and was instantly back on his bed in his room at the castle. He took several labored breaths and sat up and examined himself. His clothes and his hair were completely dry, but the taste of salt was still in his mouth.

Had he fallen asleep; was that some kind of dream? Not knowing what to think, Khan shrugged it off and walked over to his large armoire. It was almost time for the ceremony. He needed to get dressed. After staring for a few minutes at the selection, he finally picked out a navy blue tailed suit and quickly put it on. He struggled to decide whether or not to take his sword. Finally, he decided not to take it and walked out of the room. Khan strolled down the corridor, and into the throne room. He made his way over to where Lukas sat. Khan still couldn't forgive Lukas, but that didn't mean he had to hold a grudge.

There was nothing more Lukas could have done to find Drea. Khan knew that deep down. Something inside Khan knew that Drea was still alive. He just needed to make sure she was safe.

Khan pushed his melancholy thoughts aside, listened to the joyful music, and watched the people sing and dance along. Several people joined in with the dancing, even Lord Ragnar and Lady Helene took a few turns on the open floor. Khan scoffed. He knew that he neither had the heart nor the coordination to dance. He had two left feet and couldn't dance even if his life depended on it. So, instead, he closed his eyes and focused on the music, letting it take him to another realm.

Khan sang along with the chorus of voices as they sang:

"The sounds of flight echo true,

Ahoy! Here we be,

Together on the wind,

Brindles that hold the golden view,

Hold us with your faith,

O sweet dragonkin."

Khan sat down as everyone still stood and sang, his voice was getting tired. The song was about the connections man has with Dragons. However, that connection ended almost thirty years ago, when The Great King Dolion killed his dragon for fear of it becoming too powerful for him to control. That is why King Dolion is often referred to as the Dragon Slayer. Now, he understood the real truth behind the soldiers coming into Orinshire. Suddenly, a thought crossed Khan's mind. What if it was King Dolion who took Drea? What if he's torturing her, hurting her? His thoughts were broken by an eruption of applause once the music ended.

Khan watched with anticipation as Lord Ragnar and Lady Helene stood. They held their hands high.

"We have opened a trade route with the White Bridge Kingdom!" Announced Lord Ragnar.

Khan almost had to cover his ears as the room exploded with applause and happy jubilation. Eventually, even Khan joined in with the cheers as the people beside him trilled and shouted.

Chapter V

A Loose Arrow

Drea left the ceremony halfway through the songs and made the swift journey back to her room, where she changed clothes and gathered her weapons. She held her bow and quiver tightly to keep it from making sounds. Drea hurried along the long hallway with Gael in pursuit, her claws clicking against the palace floor. Drea's heart thumped inside her chest as she moved to a concealed spot, where she could observe the throne room and the people in it.

Her hands and body shook violently as she gazed down and saw her target chatting with Lady Helene.

This was all wrong. Lukas was here. Why was he here?! With one glance, he'd recognize her and come for her. Her fear and caution drove her. It allowed her to slip in unnoticed.

Her heart ached at the thought that Lukas had never come for her. She felt in her gut that he had to have known where she was. And what about Khan? Where was he? Fear clutched her mind as she wondered what happened to him. Drea pushed away the scared and nervous thoughts so she could focus. She pulled her bow off of her shoulder and drew an arrow out of her quiver and nocked the arrow on the bow string. She pulled the string back and touched the side of her lips, waiting for the right moment. She let out a groan when her shoulder twinged with a sharp pain.

Out of the corner of her eye, she saw Lukas come into view at the edge of the corridor.

Before she released the arrow, Drea looked to her left side and saw several guards running toward her. Gael whined, tucked her tail between her legs and edged closer to Drea, she could feel the dog shaking.

She ignored the oncoming soldiers, let out a slow breath and released the arrow. Just as she released the arrow, a hand slammed into the side of her shoulder, which altered the direction of the arrow. She shoved the person away, and watched the arrow in a panic. But when the arrow hit its intended target, she let out a sigh of relief. Immediately, she was surrounded by palace guards and was slammed down on the floor.

Everything went black as her head connected with the marbled stone.

❄❄❄

Drea woke up sometime later with her head pounding. She groaned as she sat up, holding her head in her hands. She rubbed her temples and tried to recall the previous event. She looked around the room. She was in a dimly lit area, the walls were brown and rust colored with large metal bars as a door. Two soldiers stood guard on either side of the door. Drea drew in the silence and began to panic. Where was Gael? Surely they hadn't taken her. She searched around the room in a blind rage. Gael had to be here.

"You're in a perfect storm. You know that, right?" Said a voice from the other side of the bars.

Drea gasped and turned toward the door. Lukas stood there, his eyes angry and his arms crossed. She looked him over, his gray hairs had multiplied.

"You've gotten old." Remarked Drea swiftly as she stood up straight. "So have you." Lukas replied.

Drea frowned. That was meant to be offensive. Her head pounded as she walked closer to the bars. The way Lukas looked at her made her uneasy. His gaze was so full of disappointment. Drea guessed that because of what she had done she wasn't going to get out of this easily.

"Yeah, well, I've already been dealt a bad hand." Drea replied to his 'perfect storm' remark. She stepped up to the bars but withdrew as she saw another man sitting back in the corner behind Lukas. The man's eyes shone in the light, his face full of disbelief and sadness. The man wasn't a man, but a boy around her age. She backed away from the door as the boy walked up to the bars beside Lukas. His golden, green eyes sparkled against the firelight.

"Khan?" Whispered Drea as she hung her head.

Drea held her breath as she heard her brother take a deep breath in reply. She looked at him, surprised when all he said was,

"Drea?"

She considered his face, his jaw was clenched. So he was mad at her. This made her uneasy as he stared at her.

"You've changed your hair." Said Khan, his voice had an edge. Drea nodded as she looked away, this wasn't the Khan she was used to. He seemed different, but she couldn't place what was different. Though, nothing else about him seemed different. Except his height, and maybe his face had changed some over the last few months. It was more defined than before.

Drea figured she seemed different to him, too, but he wasn't one to notice differences unless they were right under his nose. Drea couldn't help but feel cold as she smiled while she thought of Lord Ragnar.

"How's his Lordship? Still alive, I assume."

Lukas glared at her, his brown eyes glinting. Drea gripped her other hand as hard as she could to keep it from shaking. She sighed and broke away from his gaze.

"If he wasn't, you'd be dead."

Drea couldn't help but shiver at the thought of death. Though, the business she was in, death was around every corner. She had a right to be afraid of it, everyone did. Just then, the thought of Gael crossed her mind, but it was too late. Lukas and Khan were already walking away. She ran toward the bars and gripped the cold, steel bars in her hands.

"Wait! Where's Gael?!" Cried Drea.

She stared after the two as they kept walking out and onto the stairs. What if they hurt her, killed her? She shook her head, they wouldn't do that… Would they?

Drea turned and walked back to the narrow cot in her cell and sat down. She held back tears, brought her knees up to her chest and hugged them tightly. Everything was brilliantly going wrong. She wasn't supposed to get caught, nor were Lukas and Khan supposed to be here.

Had King Dolion planned for this all to happen? Did he know that Lukas and Khan were here? Did he want her to get caught so he could pin it all on her? She sighed, laid down on her side facing the wall and closed her eyes, desperately awaiting what would be a restless sleep.

❄❄❄

When Drea opened her eyes, she was blinded by the light. Where was she? The searing heat burned at her skin. She instinctively covered her eyes with her hands. She was somewhere hot and it smelled of smoke. The next thing she knew, a shadow covered the light, eclipsing her in darkness. She slowly looked up. There was a dragon directly above her. It looked directly back at her, its long wings blocking the sun from her view. She squinted with amazement at this large beast.

Its head was broad and defined and its scales were two different shades of red. It had deep, intelligent, blue eyes that seemed to pierce through the deepest parts of Drea's soul. She held its gaze for a moment then blinked, shook her head and looked away. What was happening, where was she? As she took in her surroundings, she became disoriented to time and place. On all sides of her there were many steam vents in the ground stretching out in all directions, throughout this vast land. No signs of vegetation anywhere. This place was as dry as a desert and as hot as the sun. Drea glanced back at the dragon and wiped the back of her hand across her forehead as sweat began to form due to the incessant heat.

"Is there a place we can get out of this heat?" Asked Drea, hoping the dragon could understand her.

To her astonishment, the dragon nodded and landed beside her, lowering itself to the ground. She held her breath as she circled the beast. Its intent seemed clear. It wanted her to climb up. But was this safe? She knew she couldn't stay there, the heat was too much for her. This was the only way she could see to escape the heat.

Drea stumbled up the dragon's bent legs and onto its back just beyond its wing joints. She held firm to the dragon's lean shoulders. If she stayed here any longer, she knew she would die, so she figured, *why not.* No reason she should go up in flames. She almost let out a scream as the dragon stood and shook its massive head. The dragon unfolded its wings and beat them once, twice, and a third time before rising up into the sky.

This time Drea did scream as the dragon swerved this way and that. Then the dragon plummeted down to a large sea. They descended closer and closer to the face of the water. She tugged hard on the dragon's wing joints to make it pull up, but it stayed its course and it seemed to go faster. She closed her eyes tight and held her breath just before they plunged into the dark water.

Drea awoke swiftly as a wave of water hit her in the face. She was groggy, but stood up just as another wave of cold water drenched her clothes and skin. She let out a groan. Her head began to pound, reminding her of her previous skirmish with the palace guards. She walked to a glassless window and peered out of it. Endless water expanded before her eyes. She took gasping breaths and sat down on her small, wooden board and contemplated what happened.

She didn't remember anything except when she saw Lukas and Khan. She winced as she stood once more. Pacing around the tiny room, she ran everything over again in her head. She remembered speaking to Lord Ragnar, but very briefly. She couldn't remember the exact words. She let out a small groan and gripped her head with both hands. She remembered now. She had told them everything including who had sent her, and who wanted Lord Ragnar dead. She had to leave, escape. If King Dolion finds out that she told them, she'd be on the chopping block. Drea trembled as she completed the puzzle. King Dolion would send someone to kill her.

PART III
THE WHITE SEA

Chapter I

Leona

"It is said that dragons roam the sea. They are those that make the billows roll. Heave ho, lads. Hold firm to your lines. *Leona* will see us through this storm." commanded Captain Damion Dale.

Khan triple knotted his rope to hold firm, so the sails wouldn't release and force the ship to go off course or crash into a hidden reef or shallow sand. As soon as he finished his knot, he moved on to the next sail. The weather had been this torturous for three days now. There was no telling how long this storm would last.

Once Captain Dale gave a command, every free hand on deck ran about the ship in a frenzy to do his duty and secure the sails before the next storm hit. It was a relentless storm, no man rested fully on the ship. Some of the men feared that syrens and monstrous sea dragons would come aboard while they all slept in their cots and hammocks below deck. Khan heard them call this place the White Sea. Its name did it justice with all the white caps. This sea was known for being rough on ships. Khan grinned when he saw Gael thundering around the deck, catching raindrops in her mouth. His thoughts drifted to Drea. She was kept in the brig in the belly of the ship. Why did she have to do this? Attempt to kill Lord Ragnar? If only it had been Khan who was taken instead of her, he would give anything to have the old Drea back.

"Khan!"

Khan jerked away from his post and glanced toward Lukas, who was standing by the Captain. Khan quickly looked over his knots and pulled them tight before heading over. Lukas and Captain Dale looked distraught. Khan swallowed down a lump in his throat and wondered what could have happened.

"She killed a guard." Stated Lukas, shaking his head in dismay.

"I'm sure she didn't mean to. She could have been provoked by the guard. *Or* possibly self-defense?" Khan suggested, hoping he was right. He sighed as Lukas and Captain Dale glared at him and shook their heads. The two men headed down the steps that led toward the brig. Khan reluctantly followed Lukas. Gael almost tripped him bolting after Lukas. Khan shivered as he entered the bottom of the ship, he was soaked to the bone. Lukas stopped, held up a hand, before placing something in Khan's palm. He glanced at it, it was a pocket knife. Khan glared at Lukas in shock. Lukas seemed determined to think the worst of Drea.

"Just in case," Lukas said before patting Khan's shoulder and walking out with the Captain.

Anxiously, Khan entered the brig and approached Drea's cell door. He didn't want to end up like the jailer. Gael was whining and pressing her nose through the bars, searching for Drea. Khan almost jumped out of his skin as he saw a hand come through the bars and scratch Gael's head. Drea's voice was barely audible as she whispered to Gael.

"Drea." Said Khan, struggling to disguise his concern. He hated to see Drea treated like this. This was his twin sister. The only family he had left and she was in a cell. As the light hit her face, he could see the anger in her eyes. Her hair was unkempt and her face and clothes were tattered and dirty.

"What? Not used to seeing people in rags anymore, are you." Remarked Drea as she stood and hung her arms out of the bars. He took a quick step back, careful to keep clear of her hands. He felt queasy as he saw several spots of blood across her clothes and some on her hands. How could she become this person? Full of hate and anger, no longer gentle and sweet. A hunter, a killer. Through the anger and hate, Khan could make out a flicker of fear on her face. He shivered as he stepped up to the bars. A thought slipped into his head as he remembered he was trained by Lord Ragnar's soldiers. He was confident he could hold her off.

As Khan came all the way up to the bars, Drea took a step back, Khan was almost a head taller than her. To his surprise, she shied away and slithered back into the safety of the cell. Khan shook his head and paced a few feet from the cell. He signaled the guard to leave. The guard acknowledged him, stood and walked away.

"Drea… Why are you doing this?" Khan asked, when he turned back to the cell. Shortly after he asked the question, Drea's knuckles connected with his nose. Khan staggered away in pain. Blood dripped from his nose. This wasn't going the way he thought it would. He grabbed a handkerchief from his back pocket and pressed it to his nose.

Drea glared at him. The fierce look of fear and anger in her eyes reminded Khan about their cat, Ariela. This is how she would watch him when she was upset with him. He glanced down at his feet. She shouldn't have to be scared of him. He sighed and shook his head, looking back to Drea.

Tears were shining in her eyes.

"You don't understand." She growled, crossed her arms and looked away from him.

"Then help me to understand Drea! I'm here, I can help you." Responded Khan as he grabbed the bars of the cell.

"I have to get away from this place. I can't be here. They'll come for me." Shuddered Drea as she walked up to the bars. "Who?" Urged Khan. Anxiety growing inside of him as he was held in suspense.

"The hunters." Said Drea as her face lost all emotion.

Khan barely had to react before she flung her hands out of the cells and her fingers wrapped around his throat.

Khan grabbed at her hands, struggling to peel her fingers from his throat. He dug his elbow into her forearm, all it did was make her tighten her grip.

Darkness started to close in as she pulled him closer to the bars. "I'm sorry," Drea whispered in his ear.

Khan choked as he tried to speak. Drea didn't budge. The last thing Khan saw before the dark closed in around him was a guard and Lukas running toward him.

❄❄❄

Khan woke up with a start. Lukas and Captain Dale sat there beside his bed. They appeared very solemn as they looked from one another and then at him. His throat throbbed painfully when he touched it.

"What happened?" Demanded Khan, his voice cracking violently as he glared at them.

"Drea attacked you."

"I know that! What else happened?" Snapped Khan as he slid his feet off the cot and onto the cold floor. "Well…" Hesitated the Captain before saying, "You've been asleep for a day. Since then, Drea's tried to escape again. She killed another guard…"

Khan let out an exhausted sigh and rubbed his temples. "Khan…" Started Lukas. Khan glanced up at him, there was sadness and guilt in his voice.

"She's beat up pretty bad." Finished the Captain while he hung his head. "She went crazy. The men didn't know how to react other than using brute force against her."

Khan stood up and glared fiercely at the two. Lukas ignored his gaze, while the Captain stared up at him apologetically. Khan shook his head, weaved his way between them and headed to the door. He heard Lukas and Captain Dale exchange a word before they got up and followed after him.

"Drea told me she needed to get away. She said that 'the hunters' were going to come for her." Explained Khan as they made their way up to the deck.

"The hunters? What hunters?" Asked the Captain when he came up to Khan's left side.

"I don't know. She didn't exactly elaborate." Said Khan as he rubbed his aching throat.

"We need to set her free. It's the only way we will be able to protect her." Stated Khan. He headed down the steps to the brig, taking two at a time. As he descended, he heard Lukas and Captain Dale immediately disagree.

Khan quickly turned and shut the door behind him, to keep them from following. Captain Dale and Lukas didn't like the idea of releasing Drea allowing her to run free around the ship. He ignored the shouts and threats that Captain Dale and Lukas spewed at him. The guards, who were keeping close eyes on Drea, stared him down.

"No one is allowed in to see her, boy." Growled a guard as he stepped toward them. Anger flared inside of Khan. In a flash, Khan whipped out his fist, ignoring the horrible, dull pain in his knuckles as they connected with the guard's face. In a few seconds, they turned on Khan. Khan backed away as they cracked their knuckles and glared at him. He gulped, and thought that maybe this wasn't such a good idea after all.

All of a sudden, a great gust of wind slammed into Khan's back, forcing him forward. After the wind died, there was a loud slam as though something heavy hit the floor.

"Don't you hurt him!" Shouted Lukas, jumping in front of Khan.

In disbelief, Khan noticed the door off its hinges and on the floor. *How in the world did it get there?* Wondered Khan as Captain Dale stood there in shock, staring at the fallen door as if he had seen a ghost.

"Uh, stand down." Stammered Captain Dale as he stepped over the door and into the brig.

The guards huffed and took a few steps back. Lukas gestured for the guards to give him the key. He could barely believe his eyes as Lukas placed the keys in his hand. Khan mouthed a thank you before walking over to Drea's cell. His heart pounded as he set the key in and turned it. He almost jumped when he heard it click, then opened the door and walked in.

Drea was lying on her bed facing the wall. As he touched her shoulder, she flinched away from him and looked up. Khan winced and felt sick in the pit of his stomach once he saw her. Her lips were cracked and swollen, and her nose was broken and bloodied. A black eye was covered by her dirty hair. Bruises dotted her arms. Khan guessed that half of her body was bruised and hurt. His eyes trailed to her feet. Both feet looked okay. Except from scars on her right ankle.

A memory flashed into Khan's mind. When he and Lukas found her being almost drowned by a crocodile, Khan almost lost her that time, he wouldn't lose her this time. Slowly and gently, Khan picked

Drea up into his arms. He angled his body so he could get out of the cell without hurting Drea. The guards, Lukas and Captain Dale watched him carry her out.

Khan turned to the guards.

"Who did this?" He asked, letting Lukas take Drea from him.

The guards shrugged and looked away from Khan. Khan scoffed madly and walked after Lukas. Whoever did this was going to pay.

Chapter II

The Whales

A bright light shone through the water's surface, illuminating the colorful sea below. Cordelia, a young Sea dragon, slithered through the water as if it were made of air. She slowed to a halt as a pod of whales swam in front of her. The whales never ceased to amaze Cordelia. Their whale song was full of beautiful words and harmonies, speaking about the days of old, definitely before Cordelia's time. As she neared the whales, they pulled away from her in panic as something small quickly made its way above the surface. Curious, Cordelia slowly swam to just below the surface. She stopped as she met her reflection. Her scales were a series of different shades of blue, and her snout was the lightest shade of blue it could go without turning gray. Along her jawline were small spines with clear, thin flesh connecting them, like that of a flying cod's wings, that extended from each side. And small gills, barely visible beneath the webbed spines. Though not many Sea Dragons have nostrils like Cordelia, all of them had gills. Cordelia was special, in that she could breathe in the water and out of the water with no difficulty.

Small black horns jutted out from the space between her ears. They rose up from her head with a slight curve and stopped about an inch or two past the length of her ears. Her eyes were gold and sparkled against the shimmering water. Her talons and feet were webbed, like a duck's feet, which made it much easier to swim. Still looking at her reflection, she slowly extended her wings from her body and closely examined them. Each wingtip was barbed and sported a long, black hook.

Her father, Sere, would always say that Cordelia looked like her mother, who sadly died when Cordelia was just a drakainling. She had suffered greatly at the hands of cruel men.

No waterling was allowed to travel to the surface. Not even the elders were allowed up there. Only the Monarch was allowed, and it was only for the meetings of the other Flights. Flights are what the dragon clans were called. Cordelia felt bad for the dragons that lived on the surface. They have to find a way to live with man, and with their rules.

The mason, who had been the waterling teacher, once said, "Men are creatures who walk above the sea; that steal from our sea."

A familiar distant call came from the Grove of Reed, pulling Cordelia from her thoughts. She sighed and looked at her reflection once more before gliding away to answer her friend's call.

❄❄❄

Bryne and Cordelia raced down the Taewe, a steep drop down into Waterling territory. Bryne was a deep green colored waterling with black eyes and large wings. Bryne and Cordelia were best friends for as long as she could remember.

"I'll get there before you!" Bryne trilled, her gentle voice barely audible above the rushing sound of water.

Cordelia disagreed swinging her tail this way and that. Her wings flapped with a fast, rhythmic beat, rocketing her ahead of Bryne. The Waterling watched in dismay when Cordelia glided past her, leaving a thick trail of bubbles.

"Cordelia! That's cheating! *You cat-fish!*" Joked Bryne and bolted after her friend.

❄❄❄

"You must learn not to go the easy way." said Sere, Cordelia's father, as he circled her.

Cordelia searched for words to explain, but only a tempered squeal escaped her lips. A lump rose in Cordelia's throat, and Bryne's face was unmistakably singing with laughter. Bryne had gotten ahead of Cordelia and pulled up right at the last moment before she hit a field of coral. Cordelia was now stuck under a large patch of fire coral. She'd have burns for days.

In shame, Cordelia lowered her head as her father and Baylor, another dragon she and Bryne had known their whole life, snapped the coral with their strong claws and teeth.

"You're too big to play in the fire coral, Cordelia." Laughed Baylor as he pulled free the last piece of coral.

Cordelia glared at him, ashamed she was found like that in front of him. His face dropped as she swam freely away. Bryne followed at a good distance behind her. Every waterling knew Cordelia was known for her hot head and quick temper.

She was also known for being the fastest swimmer. Before a Sea Dragon can truly become a Waterling, they must complete a myriad of challenges. Cordelia passed them all with ease. Baylor too, but apparently he was the Waterling prodigy. Cordelia couldn't even figure out how, maybe by his good looks, but even that would be stretching it.

Every dragon had a type of distinct power. Cordelia didn't know what hers was yet, neither did Bryne or Baylor. The three had grown up together in these depths and great coral fields. They've never been able to use their Dragonfire. Dragonfire is what makes a dragon a dragon; without it, dragons would just be big water snakes with legs and wings. Cordelia shook her head clear and slithered away.

❄❄❄

Early the next morning, Cordelia woke with a panicked start as whispers penetrated her mind and sounded in her ears.

"The King of Dragons shall not be denied. For without him, dragon-kind shall fall and die at the hands of Man."

Fear engulfed her, it was not a good sign among dragon kind to hear whispers of prophecy. Cordelia and every dragon she knew was brought up to believe that the King of Dragons would be the downfall of dragons. This couldn't mean anything good. Sere glanced at her, his eyes flicking with a questioning stare.

"Are you alright, Clam?"

Cordelia smiled at the name, she hasn't been called that in a long time. She guessed her father was feeling kinder today, — *of all days.* Cordelia nodded and sat up in her nest of seaweed.

"Uh, Sere?" Cordelia asked, twirling a piece of seaweed with her small talons.

Sere glanced at her, his mouth parted, about to answer.

"Can you tell me the meaning of the King of Dra---" Cordelia started but was swiftly cut off.

"Never mention that name!" Sere roared, rounding on his daughter.

Cordelia let out a trilling roar as she quickly swam around her father and out of the cave at lightning speed. Her heart was in her throat as she stopped in the Forest of Coral.

Why did Sere get so angry at the mention of the King of Dragons? Surely, the King of Dragons wasn't that horrible. She let out a hiss as she bumped into a sharp piece of coral that touched the burns she recently endured with the fire coral.

"Cordelia? What are you doing here?" Called a familiar voice.

Cordelia turned and let out an inward sigh of relief when she saw Baylor making his way through the coral to her. His eyes were full of concern but there was something else Cordelia couldn't place. Cordelia was about to speak, when an abnormal scent hit her nose. Baylor stared at her. Fear and panic washed over his features when Cordelia looked to where Baylor had just come from.

"Baylor, what's over there?" She whispered.

Cordelia saw a slight shudder run through Baylor when she swam closer to him. Baylor slid in front of her before she passed him. Annoyance filled her head. No way was Baylor going to challenge her. Cordelia looked one way and went the complete opposite. Baylor appeared in front of her every time.

"Baylor. Get. Out. Of. My way." Hissed Cordelia.

Baylor braced himself, obviously knowing what was coming next. Cordelia decided to surprise him.

"Oh, whatever. Forget it. Let's go catch some sharks." She trilled, masking her anger with a smile and a happy tone.

Baylor let out a loud sigh of relief, barely audible, as Cordelia swam away from him. She slowed to let him catch up. The dragon seemed to be scared of Cordelia, especially after she threatened him a little bit. One single thought remained. What was Baylor hiding in the Forest of Coral?

❄❄❄

When night had eclipsed the cove, Cordelia slowly crept around her father so she wouldn't have to answer any questions if he woke up to her leaving. Now was the time for Cordelia to find out what Baylor was hiding. On top of all this, Bryne was nowhere to be found, either by her or any other dragon. She had no possible idea of where Bryne could be.

She hadn't seen her since the fire coral incident. In the cover of night, she slithered her way toward the Forest of Coral.

She had to find out what Baylor was hiding. As she weaved through the coral, the same odd scent from earlier hit her nose once more. Cordelia followed the scent to the end of Forest of Coral. It continued down a dark ledge. She gulped as she looked down into it.

This was the Drop of Keld. It had been etched in her mind from an early age. This was a forbidden place and no dragon but one, had ever gone down into this place. He never returned…

Why had Baylor come from this direction? Cordelia thought as she slowly made her way down. Thin ribbons of blood slowly drifted up toward the surface. Fear and reason tugged at her tail, trying to get her to go back up. She left reason and continued on. A small cave stretched out to the left of her. She went in for a closer look. Shocked at the scene that lay in front of her, she gasped in horror, and thundered away from the horrible sight.

Cordelia tried hard to get the gruesome picture out of her mind as she frantically made her way back to the Forest of Coral. As she neared the edge of the Forest of Coral, Baylor slammed into her. She let out a trill of pain. The drake was freezing cold. Cordelia quickly slipped away before Baylor recovered. She watched him from behind a large piece of coral. The Waterling looked confused as to what had just happened. Cordelia hoped he assumed he hit a piece of coral. She watched as he continued on his journey and disappeared down the Drop of Keld. Cordelia swam toward home as fast as lightning.

She slowed as she neared Lonely Grove. This was a safe place just before the Waterling territory. Waterling territory was just beyond the ledge.

She shook her head as pain gripped it and it began to pound. The water around her stilled and a vision appeared before her eyes:

There was a cliff, and at the bottom of it, a large, feathered dragon laid broken on a bed of rocks. Its blood enchanting the water with a dark crimson tinge that led into the sea. Then another image replaced this one. A small egg slowly made its way down through the water.

The egg disappeared as a pod of whales swam by it. Finally, she saw a cave near Waterbed Ridge.

That was the last image she saw before blackness took over her vision.

❄❄❄

Cordelia woke to the faces of several elders, her father being among them. She looked around, wondering how she got into the elder's cave. She distinctly remembered being by Lonely Grove. Fear overwhelmed her as she noticed the Monarch staring at her, his eyes full of sorrow. She had only seen this look when a dragon had died.

She opened her mouth to speak, but she couldn't even manage a squeak before the Monarch's talons looped around Cordelia's throat. She gasped, pulling at the Monarch's arms. He was choking her! What had happened to make the Monarch so cruel? She glanced at Sere, and her father looked away from her. Her crying chokes made his chin quiver. Cordelia took gasping breaths. The Monarch let go and stormed off. An elder slowly came over, her giant talons gently cupping Cordelia's head into her hands. Her blue eyes sank deep into sadness.

"You were found near the Forest of Coral. Bryne's body was found in the Drop of Keld." The elder whispered into Cordelia's ear.

Cordelia let out mournful cries that rippled the water around her. The horrifying image of what she had seen crept back into her mind. She had seen several sharks eating up a dragon's body. But she didn't know it was Bryne's. Bryne's life had barely begun. She was Cordelia's best friend. Now, Bryne was a part of the sea and the stars beyond. She unleashed a roar of agony that echoed through the cave and out into the sea. A thought reached her mind, anger tore away at the agony.

"Cordelia. You are being charged with treason. You are suspected of having killed the Monarch's daughter." The elder said, sorrow heavy in her voice.

Cordelia glanced at her, and the anger melted into despair. No words could describe what she felt. Why would anyone assume or even think that Cordelia would kill the very dragon she grew up and practically lived with? Cordelia would never harm a scale on Bryne's back.

"Who found me?" Cordelia growled. The elder shivered at Cordelia's tone and drew away.

"Baylor did."

Cordelia shoved her way out of the cave and flew through the water at a miraculous speed.

Anger and revenge strengthened her resolve. Baylor had to pay for what he did. She would make sure of it!

Chapter III

Water & Fire

Drea stared at herself in the mirror. Her cuts were beginning to heal and most likely would end up as scars. Drea had suffered a broken rib and a sprained ankle at the hands of the guards. At least Khan and Lukas were doing everything they could to find out which guards did it. She was moved into Khan's room, which was quite spacious. Much more than she or Khan deserved. It felt weird to be in his company again, but it also felt peaceful.

She was conflicted. She didn't know whether to jump ship or stay with Khan, where she felt safe. Then again, she didn't feel safe anywhere.

Drea inhaled deeply and struggled to hold back tears as she walked back to the soft bed in the corner of the room. As she lay down, her thoughts finally decided to let her be for once. Drea was, for the first time in a long time, able to fall asleep easily.

❄❄❄

Drea jumped out of the bed and looked around. She shivered, not out of cold, but out of dread, as a voice rang through the air.

"In time, you will see what you were meant to be."

She hated hearing the whispers, it made her feel unsafe, like she was going crazy or that she was a target of some kind. She stared out the window of the cabin. It was still late in the night. She rubbed her face, took a sip of water from a small glass that was placed on the nightstand beside the bed. She climbed back in, and slipped under the warm covers once again. Drea shut her eyes peacefully. Sleep swiftly, but gently whisked her away.

❄❄❄

Drea awoke rested the next morning. The light hurt her eyes a little. She sat up, she took off her covers and planted her bare feet on the cold, wooden floor. A cold blast of wind came from the door as it opened. Drea crossed her arms awkwardly as she looked at Khan standing there uncomfortably.

He was frozen in his spot. He had not meant to wake Drea up. His hair hung over his eyes and all of his clothes were dripping wet and making puddles on the floor. Drea tried to stifle a laugh as she took in his appearance.

"Uh, glad you find this funny." Said Khan with an odd smile.

Drea looked away, covering her smile as Khan walked around her and into their room and shut the door.

Drea let out a sigh and gently rubbed her broken rib. It throbbed quite a bit, and it was probably the worst wound she had ever suffered. She could still feel the effects of the concussion she endured at Lord Ragnar's palace. There remained a slight bump on the back of her head and a dull persistent headache. She sighed as she saw her reflection in Khan's watery footprints. The next thing she knew her reflection turned to fire. Alarmed, she stepped back from the watery footprints and rubbed her eyes. Maybe it was the concussion, or just her mind playing tricks on her?

❄❄❄

Drea limped toward Khan and Lukas. Both were eagerly waiting for her on the main deck of the ship. Gael followed her quickly, and she was eager to see her master. Drea groaned to herself as she saw Captain Damion Dale, the ship's captain, turn toward her. He seemed to share her disgust as he awkwardly looked away and struck up a conversation with Lukas. Khan hesitantly approached her with his hands behind his back. She couldn't help but let out a soft laugh as Gael stopped his pursuit by jumping up on him and pawing at his chest. Khan tenderly petted the dog's head and spoke kind words to her. Drea couldn't help but wonder what Khan had gone through before they were reunited. Had he seen more visions like Drea? More dragons?

"Hey," Said Khan, giving Drea an awkward smile.

"Hi." Offered Drea.

As Khan and Drea conversed, Lukas had swiftly gotten himself into an argument. It didn't take much to stop it, however, as Drea marched right in between Lukas and Captain Dale. She faced the Captain and pushed him roughly by the shoulders taking him off guard, causing him to stumble.

The Captain put his arms up in surrender, walked slowly backward and left. Drea let out a snort. Her heart dropped as she turned to see Khan's and Lukas's faces full of disappointment.

"What?" Scoffed Drea as she walked back to Khan.

"That young man is the only reason you are still alive. You're lucky; he's a great deal more respectable a Captain than we've come across lately." Remarked Lukas, a hint of reprimand seasoning his words.

Drea looked at Khan, waiting for him to speak up for her. Khan let out a sad sigh and shook his head, obviously agreeing with Lukas. Drea, clearly disappointed at his response, felt her cheeks reddening and her ears burning. She sighed and hung her head, as she had done when she was younger. Getting scolded by her brother was the most embarrassing thing ever. Lukas's glare just made her feel like she was worth less than a bronze coin. She swallowed down a lump in her throat and followed behind Khan as Lukas led the way.

Drea gripped the railing as a loud burst of thunder roared and a crack of lightning flashed across the sky. It startled her. She had never seen a storm like this before. The rain started coming down heavier now. Drea shivered, struggling to keep her teeth from chattering from the cold. She groaned after turning too quickly causing her rib to smart. She felt relief as she saw Khan step back to her. That feeling quickly disappeared as Lukas took hold of the collar of Khan's shirt and whispered something in his ear.

Drea looked on with sadness when they both continued up the steps. How cruel would Lukas continue to be? She didn't hurt him, or at least she didn't think she had. She let out a sigh and stumbled after them. She couldn't help but feel isolated and alone. Khan glanced back at her, with concern as Lukas guided him forward. Drea looked up at the sky. The rain had begun to taper off. Almost immediately, Lukas shot up the stairs, leaving Khan and Drea alone on the steps. Khan sighed and took Drea's arm in his and helped her make her way up the steps.

"We'll have to make do with this, Damion." Said Lukas as Drea and Khan came out onto the deck.

The Captain nodded and shouted beside Lukas, instructing each man on deck to get to work. The crew immediately started to unfurl the sales in response to the Captain's command. Drea watched in surprise as the Captain hustled over to an elderly man struggling to pick up a heavy barrel. It sure surprised Drea that such an obnoxious man can be selfless at times. Khan seemed to notice her attention on the Captain and pulled her to a corner of the deck.

"Damion, honestly, isn't that bad. He's not like you think." Said Khan.

Drea considered him, surprised her brother would defend such a man. He had allowed Drea to get beat up by his men and let them get away with it. Khan searched her face and frowned.

"He has the ones responsible for hurting you in chains and behind bars." Said Khan as he let go of her arm and walked away to start helping.

Drea couldn't understand how her brother could admire the Captain. Her attention back on the chaos on the deck, she was shocked to see the Captain staring at her as if she were supposed to be helping. She let out a disgusted groan and stumbled away.

❄❄❄

During the night, Drea awoke to the smell of smoke. She coughed as she opened her eyes to find smoke sneaking under a crack in the door. Where was Khan? Drea gasped for air as a pair of hands grasped her throat and held her down on her bed. Desperate for air, she fought the hands holding around her neck. The cabin was on fire. Her lungs screamed for air as the fire illuminated the attacker's face. Fear rippled through her when she recognized the broad face of Jax.

He was a notorious killer, never turning down an assignment, no matter who he had to eliminate. Darkness began to rim Drea's vision as pounding and banging sounded at the door. She let out one last breath as the door flew open and darkness overtook her.

❄❄❄

Khan stumbled through the smoke in a blind haze, he had to find Lukas. He had left his cabin early in the morning. A few hours after sunrise, Khan smelled smoke and had made his way to the cabins at the bottom of the ship that held all the men and workers. Khan had made sure everyone was accounted for and instructed them to abandon the ship. All but Drea, Lukas and Captain Dale were accounted for. He had gone through every cabin, every passage. The three were nowhere to be found. Just as he was about to enter the last hallway, a loud voice rang out in the air.

"Khan!"

Khan jerked toward the voice and saw Lukas and Captain Dale. He gasped as he saw Drea limp in the Captain's arms. Lukas was staring at him, gesturing for him to follow. Khan took a step forward and let out a scream as he was rocketed backward. The floorboards on the top deck directly in front of him exploded. Khan was flung through the air and away from the ship into the frigid waters.

The last thing he felt as darkness took over his vision was the hard surface of a wooden board that had been blown from the ship, against the back of his head and the cold sensation of water.

Chapter IV

An Unexpected Savior

Drea awoke with a desperate need for air. She sat up in a daze gasping, and grabbed at the Captain's reaching hands as he tried to settle her. She couldn't speak! Her throat burned and ached as she tried to talk. It came out as muffled pitiful squeaks. Captain Dale shook his head and put a finger to his lips. Drea obeyed as she surveyed the room. Lukas was sleeping fitfully in a chair, opposite her bed, his face a mask of agony. As she looked closer at Lukas, she could see two gaping wounds. One on his right shoulder and the other on his left hip.

Drea wanted to ask what had happened, but thought better of it and said nothing. Captain Dale looked at Drea, understanding her unasked question.

"You've been asleep for two days. Lukas was injured trying to rescue you. Your attacker had a knife and Lukas did not. It's pretty bad." Said the Captain.

Drea looked around the room once more. She sat up straighter when she didn't see anyone else in the room but the three of them. She sent a worried glance back toward the Captain. He seemed to already know what her next question would be if she could speak. Somehow, deep down, Drea already knew the answer. The Captain hung his head as he stood up and walked away.

Drea let out a gentle sob, bringing her knees to her chest. She buried her face in her arms and allowed herself to cry. Khan was gone.

❄❄❄

The sound of seagulls calling and the faint swish of white-capped waves falling on the shore filled the air. Khan slowly opened his eyes, propped himself up with his elbows and looked around. He groaned as his whole body began to ache. He shut himself up when he heard a slight trill echo through the cavern where he had been taken. Khan sat up and peered into the shadows. His heart quickened as he noticed something hunched over in the darkness. Dread clung to his heart once he began to hear the faint cries of a young girl. As he stood, the thing stood up with him. Khan froze when it slowly slithered toward him.

Before he could make out what it was, slimy hands slithered over his eyes and covered his mouth. Khan struggled against the power and pushed back. He heard a burst of music as the hands released him. He stumbled out of the cave and into the crisp air. Panic pulled Khan farther and farther away from the cave. Khan tried to make sense of what had just happened. Moments later a gentle melody floated through the air and into Khan's ears. He let himself relax as complex harmonies created a mellow tone and engulfed his senses. It was the most beautiful thing he had ever heard. It lured him back to the cave. Before he could step inside, a large, ear-piercing roar sounded behind him. Khan snapped out of the trance and looked up. He could make out the figure of a dragon.

His attention was turned back toward the cavern, where he saw beautiful fish-like women slithering out toward him. Khan let out a scream and dodged their webbed fingers. Syrens! They *were* real!

The dragon roared as it streaked past Khan and hunted the syrens. Khan watched intently as the dragon caught a fleeing syren in its jaws, but looked away when he heard a sickening crunch. Caught off guard, Khan lost his footing as he was being dragged into the water. Kicking and struggling, he tried to break free of the syren's grasp. He could hold his breath no longer. Water filled his lungs, he fell limp, unable to fight any longer.

The deadly creature let out a trill of triumph and released his throat for the final blow. Khan knew this was it. He closed his eyes as the syren came closer. He braced himself, then nothing. Khan opened his eyes to see the dragon tearing the syren apart. Black began to rim the edges of his vision as he struggled to the surface. He held his breath as his chest jerked, his lungs searching for air. He slowly sank, falling farther and farther away from the surface.

Something swam underneath Khan and shoved him upward. Seconds later, his whole body broke through the water's surface and landed on the shore. Khan gasped for air and coughed out the water he had swallowed. He turned back toward the water. The dragon met his gaze as it waded back to the shore. Amazed, Khan realized that the dragon had dove into the water and pushed him up to the surface and toward the shore. The dragon had saved him, but why?

The early rising sun illuminated the dragon's features. Even though he feared it, he was rather amazed by it. Khan couldn't quite describe it. Everything about it was fascinating. Its eyes were bright gold, and hundreds of scales rippled its body, each a different shade of blue. Small black horns jutted out of its skull, each wing tip had a barbed, black hook. Khan hadn't expected to ever meet a dragon. He had never even thought they were real until Lady Helene flew into the castle courtyard on the back of one. Hot steam came out of its nostrils as it let out short bursts of breath. The dragon was the size of a tall horse. He bowed his head to the dragon, unsure of what else to do.

"Thank you." He said, looking directly at the dragon.

It let out a loud, angry trill and swept its tail at Khan's ankles. He let out a grunt as he hit the sand with a thump. It roared as it launched itself upward and dived back into the water. Khan stared after it, amazed and shocked. He let out a small, shaky laugh and stood up. His knees felt like jelly.

❄❄❄

Through the light of the fire that he had just built, Khan could make out the glowing eyes of the dragon watching him from the trees. After the beach incident, Khan wasn't sure what to expect anymore. One thing he did know, he needed to find his way back to civilization. He figured he wasn't very far from the White Bridge Kingdom.

Ever since his encounter with the dragon, it seemed to never leave him. Khan was lucky it hadn't done anything to him. He had no way to defend himself if it did. Though he knew how dangerous a dragon could be, he felt safe when it was around. Comfortable even. *It'll scare everything away, hopefully everything,* he thought.

Khan felt he could trust it. It did save him, after all. Although, it was kind of unnerving for it to follow him. Perhaps it was searching for something and Khan just happened to be heading in that direction. He shook his head as he laid down beside a log and shut his eyes, that probably wasn't the case. Khan let out a discontented sigh and hoped sleep would come quickly.

❄❄❄

Early the next morning, Khan started his journey toward town. As expected, the dragon followed him. Every so often he would turn around and could see her golden eyes reflecting the sun. Khan wanted to try something but was unsure how to go about it or how the dragon would react. As the sun began to fade, he walked up to her. Khan was more amazed with her every time he saw her. The beauty of this dragon made him feel enchanted. As Khan reached out to her snout and touched it, thunder cracked, scaring the dragon. The dragon let out a trilling roar and swung her wings. In doing so, the dragon's black hook on the bend of her wing slid across Khan's face and down his neck. Khan let out a loud cry of pain as the dragon bounded away.

He pressed his hands on the wounds and dropped to the ground. The pain was excruciating. He tore his shirt apart, split it into strips and quickly wrapped his neck. The sun was beginning to sink into the earth. Khan had to find a safe place to sleep. He struggled up a tree and climbed up onto a thick branch, about halfway up. His wounds continued to bleed through the cloth and down his neck. He wiped it away with his wrist and shuddered with pain as the wounds began to throb. *This is going to be a long night,* thought Khan.

All through the night, the only thing to be heard was the gentle forest sounds. Occasionally, a lonely dog would howl, and eventually, it would get answered by several far away howls. The thing that unnerved him the most was the caterwaul of a wild cat somewhere off in the distance. He didn't fear anything more than a wild cat. They were big and ruthless. The scent of blood wouldn't help his plight either. They could also climb trees. Khan shivered when a cold, brisk wind pierced his chest through the holes in his torn shirt. Luckily, his injuries from the dragon had stopped bleeding. Though they still stung and radiated with heat. Khan was not really used to dealing with injuries. That was more Drea's thing. Sadness began to grip his heart as he thought of the others, he hoped they had better luck than him today. He didn't trust Captain Dale with Drea, who knows what they could do to each other if they got on the wrong side of things. Then again, they were always on the wrong side of things.

Khan shook his head as he laid it back on the tree and gazed up through the leaves and branches. He felt relief as the faint trace of exhaustion invaded his body and mind. Khan took one last look at the stars shimmering in the sky before shutting his eyes, wishing for a restful sleep.

❄❄❄

The sound of crackling fire roused Khan from his sleep. He gasped; he was in an unfamiliar room. He sat up and looked at himself. His shirt was gone. He jumped as he spotted himself in the mirror a few feet away. His wounds were stitched neatly together, as though someone had done it hundreds of times. Khan glanced at his face, the cut traveled from the end of his right eyelid to his bare chest. It would scar, change his face altogether. Khan stifled a cry of sadness and realized he'd never look the same again. Drea would be mortified; as would Lukas. Khan swiftly threw himself down on his pillow and shut his eyes when he heard whispers coming from the other room.

"Sh! He's awake, I tell you! Heard him meself."

"Come now, Dottie. I'm sure it was just in 'ur mind."

Khan let himself lie still as he heard the voices drawing closer and the sound of loud footsteps slowed and stopped. Khan sat up and took hold of a small knife that was on a stool next to him when he felt a hand touch his forehead. He let out a strained gasp when he saw a young girl backing away from him. She was at least six or more years younger than him. He switched the direction of the knife once another scream erupted from the open doorway. It was a woman with her hands covering her mouth. Khan let out a yell when a firm hand struck his wrist and sent the knife flying. He shoved away an older boy and backed himself to the wall so he could see all three. Will there ever be a moment when nothing would go wrong? Perhaps when he was dead, maybe? Khan let out a sigh as the boy pulled out a sword and pointed it at Khan. He couldn't help but feel sorry for the chap. He looked more scared than the other two. Another girl came up behind the younger one and pulled her away.

"Make no mistake, I never would have let you hurt them." Said a voice from the shadows.

Khan gulped when he saw a man much older than him come out from the opposite side of the room. He held back a slick arrow with a broad bow. Where was he?

"Who are you?" Demanded Khan as he stood up straight and matched the man's height when he said,

"Better question is, who are you?"

Chapter V

The Search

Cordelia trudged along the trees. She could still taste the scent of blood in the air coming from her wing tip. Something about that human boy fascinated her, that made her want to interact with him. She'd been tracking him since the beach, through the woods and valleys. She thought back to the beach after she accidentally slit his face, neck and chest with her sharp talon. She hadn't meant to do it. She was scared when thunder and lightning hit right at that moment. It was something she had never experienced before. She felt bad about what had happened.

Cordelia had been banished and dishonored, all because of a false accusation. She was able to score her talons across Baylor's broad face, and for that, she was pleased. It was a feeble attempt to avenge Bryne's life. Even if she didn't kill Baylor, she had caused him some agony, at least. It hadn't helped her case, though. If she could attack Baylor, who wouldn't think she could kill Bryne? The Monarch was quite devastated about everything. He also seemed to want Cordelia dead. Though why would he think Cordelia would kill or even attempt to hurt Bryne? Cordelia had no answer for that. If only she could have figured out why Baylor killed Bryne. She had known him her whole life. Clearly, no one knew *exactly* who he was.

Cordelia shook her head and continued on her way, she had to find this human that she had accidentally marked. She couldn't remember when she felt at peace like she did when she was with him. Cordelia let out a soft trill and shivered. She had never really experienced cold or warmth in the water. This was much more Cordelia's taste. It was almost as if she belonged above the water than in it. She picked up her pace once she found a trace of blood scent going up a tree. Cordelia gulped, it was a tall tree. She shook her head and scampered up it. Though she could fly, she wasn't very fond of heights, any type of heights for that matter. As Cordelia reached the top of the tree, a memory flashed through her mind.

Cordelia stifled a bellow of sadness as she remembered when she and Bryne would race to the Fire Coral Patch. They loved swimming through it and would occasionally get stung by the coral. Even though it hurt, it didn't change how much fun it was. Cordelia gulped down the lump rising in her throat and looked around. It was already dark. The fact that she was a dragon, didn't change the fact that there could be numerous threats to her if she continued to search in the night.

❄❄❄

Chirping and clicking woke Cordelia from her peaceful sleep on the branch. She opened her eyes to a small woodland creature gnawing on an acorn. At the sight of it, her stomach rumbled.

Cordelia let out a tired sigh, which scared the creature and bounded away from her.

A loud crack caught Cordelia's attention just before she leaped down from the tree. A human! Cordelia swiftly hugged the tree's branch with all her might. She didn't feel safe around this one, it carried a sword and multiple sticks that held pointy stones at the tip of it. Cordelia let a rumble escape her throat. The sticks looked exactly like the hooks they used to kill her mother. She gritted her teeth as the human passed under her. It took all her will not to pounce.

Cordelia felt something rising and boiling inside her chest. It burned her insides as it traveled up her throat. She opened her mouth and fixed her gaze on the human. The world went silent as a burst of boiling water rushed out of her mouth and down to the human. She tuned out the dreadful cries of the human as the water burned its skin.

She let out a bellow of pain as something sharp pierced through her scales. Cordelia turned toward the threat and let out a rumbling growl. She spotted another human hiding in the thicket. She roared, making the human take off running in the other direction. She twisted her neck and pulled out the long pole that extended from her shoulder. Cordelia extended her wings and took flight after the human and let out a shrieking roar as the human leaped onto a horse and forced it into a gallop. Cordelia followed swiftly, her wings beating loudly. She let out a roar as she saw the human heading toward a village. Cordelia picked up her pace, feeling the boiling water fill her belly once again. She trilled in exhilaration as the human made it through the archway into the town. Cordelia dove below the archway and followed. She caught the human in her jaws as she hit a large stone pillar.

After a few moments, Cordelia rose from the shattered pillar with the limp human in her jaws. Horrified screams echoed throughout the air when she let the body drop to the dirt with a thump. She bared her fangs and flattened her ears against her neck while twenty or so men with rope and weapons closed in around her.

Cordelia hissed just as the thick rope was strung around her snout and shut it tight. She thrashed this way and that, struggling to get away from the bonds she was in. Each man threw a thick rope over Cordelia to the men on the other side. As if there was no difficulty with Cordelia's size, she was pulled quickly and painfully to the ground. She let out a miserable sound as they strung together her front arms and back legs. Panic engulfed her. The men struck her with sharp, barbed sticks.

She looked up and heard a familiar voice yell ahead of her. It was the young boy she had been following. Cordelia fought back with all her might as the boy drew closer. She dropped to the ground in agony once more as one of the men shoved a heated pole into her hip.

"Stop it! You're hurting her!" The boy cried.

Cordelia rumbled in despair when she felt there was nothing else she could do. Something inside her clicked when she saw the boy she had saved being manhandled and shoved away from her. *No, no, no. Not on my watch!* Whispered Cordelia.

In defiance, Cordelia shifted her weight and brought her wing across the ropes. She was surprised at how easily it cut through them. She let out a triumphant bellow when she finally tore the rope free that was around her snout.

Everyone around her fell silent and gasped as the rope fell. Cordelia twisted her head back and laid hold onto the pole and pulled it painfully out of her hip. She stood on her hind legs, threw her head back into the air and let out an ear-piercing roar. Cordelia angrily thrust her head down to the man that had hurt the boy. Immediately, the boy jumped in front of her. He held his hands up in surrender, staring into her eyes. Cordelia gazed at the wound she caused him and peered into his eyes. It was the one she had given him a few days ago. She hoped he knew she didn't mean it. There was a look of understanding in his eyes, which made Cordelia think he did know. Immediately, she could feel a connection between her and the boy. Cordelia let out a trilling roar as the ground beneath her feet shifted and explosions sounded around the small village. Fire rained down on the village causing the buildings to be set ablaze. *Fire*. Cordelia had never seen anything like it. As she looked around the village, she saw a black dot with large wings in the sky. Another dragon? Cordelia shook her head and turned back to the village.

Her heart wrenched as she heard the deafening cries of despair and fear of people as their small village began to burn. Suddenly, a familiar scent hit her nostrils, a scent of home. Cordelia shifted her weight, she turned to gaze at a large well. Excitement coursed through her as she launched her body into the air and then dove straight into the well.

Her body seemed to tremble with joy as the water hit her flesh. She forgot how it felt to be in the water. So refreshing, clean. It reminded her of home. Cordelia swiftly filled up her belly with the sweet water as she headed back to the surface. Screams filled her ears again as Cordelia burst through the opening of the well and flew high into the air. She felt the burning sensation rising up her throat once again, causing her to release a large fume of water from her mouth, dropping it over the buildings on fire below. Cordelia thought she could hear scattered cheers as several fires were quenched.

Cordelia hovered by the broken entrance to the town. She spotted the boy who tried to save her on his knees holding his head as if he was in pain. Her heart stopped when she saw the cracks in the wound she gave him glowing bright blue. Cordelia landed down just beside the boy. He screamed in pain and fell backward. The townspeople began to turn and run to help him. Cordelia kept them away with her sharp talons. She couldn't bear the terrible sounds that the boy was making. Instinctively, she picked up the writhing boy and clutched him between her talons. Cordelia launched herself upward as a steady drizzle of rain poured down on the town.

❄❄❄

Cordelia watched over the boy for hours on end. The night came and went, the boy had not once moved from his position. She tried to sleep, but troubled thoughts kept her awake.

She felt protective over the human, for whatever the reason. Why did she feel this way? What did it mean? Cordelia laid her head on her talons and gazed at the sleeping boy. She had done what she could to keep him warm, but the cold winds weren't helping. Cordelia let out a gentle breath as she shook off the brisk wind and strained her eyes, trying to keep them open. Maybe she could just rest them for a moment or two? Cordelia shut her eyes and was overtaken with sleep.

❄❄❄

Cordelia yawned rather loudly and stretched all her limbs. Blinking away the sleep from her eyes, she took in her surroundings. In an instant, Cordelia was up on her feet, anxiously searching the area. The human was gone!

Sadness and sorrow began to overwhelm Cordelia as she sat down on the forest floor with a thump. Cordelia bared her teeth, giving in to her frustration. A moment later, she heard a sound behind that made her jump.

An old man and a young woman slowly came out of the bushes with their palms out to her. Cordelia let out a chirp as a cold hand touched her shoulder. She felt relief as she saw another face beside her. It was the boy! She gazed down at him in sympathy, he looked ill.

"Easy. Easy." Said the boy, gently patting her snout when she brought it down to him.

"Surely, this cannot be the friend you were looking for?"

Cordelia let out a trilling growl as she faced the older man and woman who stood gaping at her. They both took a few steps back out of fear.

"*Cat-fish.*" Growled Cordelia, even though she knew they couldn't understand her.

"Ha, no. They're not really." Said the boy beside her as he watched the two back away. Cordelia gaped down at him. The boy seemed twice as shocked as he realized he had just heard a dragon speak to him. The man and woman seemed confused at what happened. Cordelia seemed to share their reactions as the boy beside her fumbled with his words, trying to talk and understand how a human could understand a dragon?

"He will guide your path as you will his."

Cordelia shuddered when the eerie voice sounded in her ear. She didn't like this. She didn't like that he understood her. She hated the voices. It made her feel unwelcome and cold. Cordelia looked at the boy. His face was a mask of confusion. As they stood there, looking at each other, the weather changed and a swift downpour scattered the last patches of warmth in the air.

"You will come to understand."

For once in her life, Cordelia was scared for her life.

PART IV
WINTER'S BEGINNING

Chapter I

Back In The Saddle

Drea walked close to Captain Dale. It was cold today. She had to press closer to him to avoid boisterous people shouldering by her. She struggled not to pull away from him as she felt his hand slip across her shoulders, guiding her away from the crowd. They were in the marketplace today in need of supplies, mostly for food than anything else. Drea would never have been able to leave camp on her own. Lukas would have never allowed it, so instead she asked the Captain to go with her. Surprisingly, Lukas agreed to let her go, but only if Captain Dale went with her. Drea resented the Captain, though he had been treating her much better than she did him.

She shivered as a gust of wind caught her hood and swiftly tore it from her head. Instantly, the Captain's free hand reached out and grabbed it before it came completely off her head. Drea couldn't help but feel grateful as he pulled the hood back down to cover her eyes and face. She stifled a groan, as he had pulled it too far down making it difficult for her to see. Now, Captain Dale would have to guide her. Drea wasn't about to chance removing her hood allowing someone to catch a glimpse of her face and turn her in.

Drea's ears focused in toward the sound of paper crumpling. It appeared to be coming from Captain Dale.

"What's that, Captain?" Drea whispered as the sound stopped.

"Just a warrant for your head. And please, call me Damion."

Drea gulped as they continued on home. Drea, Damion, and Lukas had come ashore into one of the Great King Dolion's ally's territories. Of course, he had put a price on Drea's head and told people that she was the one who tried to assassinate Lord Ragnar. Apparently, Erdale was the second strongest ally to the King and would do anything to please him.

Damion pulled Drea out of the way of a big group of soldiers. She sighed; no matter how much she disliked the Captain, he was better to her than she deserved. Why did he try so hard? Her thoughts drifted to Khan. Had he forgiven her for what she had done? Khan released her after she almost took his life. That's why she did it, to test him, to see if he'd still release her after she betrayed him.

Drea gasped and looked up as she was shoved to the ground, causing her hood to come off her head. Damion let out a hollow grunt as he too was shouldered to the ground. Drea quickly slid into a lunge, keeping herself close to the gravel. She kept two fingers on the rocky surface while her other hand reached around to her back and gripped the hilt of her small blade.

"Sorry, 'bout that mate. Watch where you're going next time." Said one of the men mockingly.

Damion groaned as he shook his head and looked up.

"Oh… Great." He said as he began to stand.

Five men stood in front of them. Each wore the kingdom's colors. Blue and white. They all had their hands on the hilts of their large swords. Drea bit back a remark to Damion as he stepped in front of her. He took a quick step back as the five men took a step toward him.

"Whoa, whoa. Easy." Stated a calm and familiar voice. Drea turned to see Lukas come up beside them. He flashed her an angry look before getting in front of Damion. Drea stood up straight as the men eased up on the grips of their swords. The captain of the squad stepped forward.

"What is your business here?" Asked the large man, his eyes lingering on Drea.

"Just here for supplies." Said Damion standing up straight as the man approached him. The man pushed past him and stopped directly in front of Drea.

"Hmm." He said as he looked her over. Just before he turned to walk back, he looked over to his left and nodded to someone.

Drea cried out in pain as an arrow flew into the back of her thigh. Damion reached her as she fell. The leader caught him by the throat and flung him away from her. The other four men closed in around Lukas but the captain stood in front of Drea. She gritted her teeth in pain as she tried to crawl away from him.

In pain, she tore the arrow from her thigh. She held it firmly in her hand. Drea stood unsteadily, wincing as she put weight on her left leg. The leader reached for her. Drea dodged and jabbed the arrow into his shoulder as he went past. The leader howled in pain and turned on her. Drea deflected his blows, crying out when the blows eventually broke past her barrier. She screamed as the leader punched his big fist into her left thigh. Drea fell to the ground in pain.

She glanced around for the others. Two of the men were on the ground unconscious. The other two battled Lukas while he defended a wounded Damion.

Drea let out a deep cry of pain as a dirty boot connected with her jaw and sent her flying face first into the dirt.

Drea was dazed from the blow, but could see the leader pull out two slender swords from their scabbards.

Drea was vulnerable to his attack. She had to protect herself. Calculating his proximity, at the last second she rolled out of the way of the shining blades and into a squatting position. Her breath came out in short, uncontrolled bursts. Drea took in her surroundings. To her left side were several crates piled up like stair steps. The leader roared as she ran toward the crates. As she climbed up on the last crate, she turned to face the man.

"You won't get out of this so easily." He hissed.

Drea closed her eyes and took a breath before opening them once again. She pulled out her small blade and dove forward. The leader let out a grunt as Drea hit him. They both hit the ground hard. After watching Drea tumble a few yards away, Lukas hurried over to help her up. When she looked up, the leader of the kill squad was getting up from the ground. He was groaning in pain and shaking as he reached for the knife that was embedded in the left side of his chest.

"Come on." Said Lukas as he pulled Drea up.

Once Drea was up and steady, Lukas turned away to Damion.

Drea was caught off guard when she saw Damion in a pool of blood with his left leg injured. She turned as she heard a sharp whinny to her right and quickly ran over to the five horses that the kill squad had left. Gently, but swiftly, Drea grabbed the reins of two horses and led them to Lukas. She watched with distress as Lukas hoisted Damion up on his shoulders and headed toward her. Stepping up to the left side of the horse, she slid her foot into the stirrup and swung her leg over the horse's saddle and into the other stirrup. Damion let out groans of pain in response to Drea and to Lukas pulling him up behind her.

"Hold onto her!" Shouted Lukas as he turned and jumped onto the other horse. He quickly urged the horse into a gallop as the soldiers started to wake up. Drea's heart pounded with adrenaline when the horse thundered forward. Exhilarated, she dug her heels into its side and urged it forward. It let out a loud whiny and eased into a fast, rhythmic gallop following after Lukas.

Drea sucked air through her teeth as her thigh began to throb. She bounced up and down with the horse's movements. Coming from their left was a large band of armored horses and soldiers heading their way.

"Faster!" Drea shrieked at the horse and felt a small tinge of relief as its speed increased again.

Damion mumbled something she couldn't make out. Her heart lurched when she felt the warmth of blood against her back. Worry overcame her as she felt Damion's grip loosen.

"Stay with me! Stay with me, Damion." She shouted over the rumbling, cold wind.

She struggled to keep him awake. As they rode, she heard a faint buzzing sound right by her head, then another and this time she felt a sharp sensation on her left ear as an arrowhead grazed it. Drea gritted her teeth and whipped the reins again and again, hoping the horse would pick up more speed. Finally, Drea caught up with Lukas. She looked at him at the same time he looked at her. At that moment, she saw his upper body jerk; she knew what happened. Lukas had been hit. She saw a thin arrow coming out of both sides of left shoulder. He let out a scream of pain and anger as the horse faltered under him. He had pulled on the reins, causing it to jerk to the side. Drea's heart lurched when she saw a large gap in a trench up ahead.

"Lukas! Look!" Shouted Drea.

"Let go of your reins! Hold onto Damion!" Shouted Lukas back.

Drea gaped at him.

"Are you insane?! We'll fall to our deaths!"

The distance between both sides of the trench had to be close to thirty feet.

Lukas looked back at her, a sincere look in his eyes, begging her to trust him. Drea groaned loudly and nodded her head. She let go of the reins and held tight to Damion's elbows.

She closed her eyes as they edged closer to the trench. She felt the horse jump. She opened her eyes when the fall never came. She and Damion let out a gasp as the horse's legs touched down on the ground and slid on its haunches once it connected with the opposite side of the trench. She and Damion were both thrown off by the impact. Drea struggled to catch her breath. She landed hard with her face in the grass and Damion on top of her. She groaned and crawled out from under him. Once she was free of his weight, she sat up and struggled to breathe, trying hard to not hyperventilate. She watched on fearfully at Lukas while his horse jumped and began to fall to its doom.

In a silent moment, something flew out of Lukas's palms that threw him upward. Drea shut out the horse's cries as it fell and hit the bottom of the trench. Lukas landed a few feet away from her, his knees and palms taking the brunt of the fall. Seconds later, Lukas was up and running toward the remaining horse and grabbed its reins. Drea stood while staring defiantly at the band of soldiers gawking at them from the other side of the trench.

The archer raised his bow high in the air and released an arrow. Drea took a faltering step back as the arrow landed two inches from her feet. One of the soldiers pulled out a horn and blew into it. The sound was deafening. Drea had to cover her ears as it echoed through the trench.

"Drea! Come on!" Hissed Lukas as he grabbed at her arm.

Drea cursed under her breath as one lone soldier stayed behind and stared at her. He wore King Dolion's colors, red and black. His face uncovered, his helmet on his hip. Drea had seen that face before. Her heart stopped. It was the man she saw that day when the King's soldiers burnt her home to ashes. Anger and sorrow gripped Drea's heart as she felt a lump begin to rise in her throat.

She turned and ran toward Lukas who helped her onto the horse before jumping up in front of Damion. She held onto him tenderly, careful of his wounds. She glanced back as Lukas, nudged the horse into a trot and let out a shaky sigh as she saw the soldier still there watching.

❄❄❄

Drea and Lukas burst through the house door, Damion hanging limp in their arms. The people inside shrieked as Lukas let go of Damion, causing Drea to slowly lay him on the wooden floor. She swiftly pressed her hands down on Damion's stomach, blood continued to come through the wound. Fear pricked Drea's heart as Damion's hands grabbed at hers in pain. She looked down at his face, his eyes slowly began to close. Drea stammered as she struggled to comfort him. Lukas yelled at the house's occupants for help. An elderly couple and two young children appeared in the doorway just before he ran back to Drea and Damion. Lukas fell to his knees, placed his hands on Drea's and applied more pressure to the bleeding wound. Drea glanced back at the scared family. The fear in their eyes matched her own.

"Please! He's dying!" She shouted as tears began to sting her eyes.

She looked away and then at Lukas, whose brow was furrowed and bloodied.

"Put your hand on his forehead. No, keep one on his stomach." directed Lukas.

Drea obeyed and Lukas did the same. She shivered as his bloodied hands laid on top of hers while he chanted something under his breath. Drea let out a cry of pain when she felt something draining out of her body through the palms of her hands. It was excruciating. She flung her head back as a spasm shook her body causing her to scream. Lukas groaned in pain in front of her, his hands struggling to stay on hers. Drea jerked as she felt a hand touch her shoulder. Looking around in surprise, she saw the family gather around them and chant something similar to what Lukas had been saying even though Drea couldn't understand. Drea's hair flung up as a gust of wind rushed through it. She shook her head as weariness took over her mind. The wind stopped along with the pain and a faint voice echoed in her head as darkness took over her vision.

"In the dry, you'll find water. In the cold, you'll find heat."

❄❄❄

A few hours later, Drea woke with a headache, her eyes blurry as she struggled to make out her surroundings. Her thigh still ached, and she was reminded of the recent events. The soft crackle of a fire echoed through the air while she took a deep breath and rubbed at her eyes. She couldn't help but feel relief when she saw Damion sleeping soundly on a small cot a foot or two away from her. Just past him she saw Lukas staring at his palms in sorrow. Lukas connected with Drea's eyes and slowly stood up and made his way to the small cot where Drea sat. She opened her mouth to ask him a question. He squatted in front of her, shushing her and gently pressing her shoulders back.

"You need to rest. You've been through quite an ordeal," Whispered Lukas. Drea didn't argue but laid her head back down on the bed and looked up at him.

Lukas stayed there a few more seconds before clearing his throat and walking away.

"Get some rest." was all he said as he left the room.

Chapter II

The Dragon

Khan walked after Alvis. He had met Alvis after the events with his scar and dragon. Alvis was an older gentleman who had once served the White Bridge Kingdom as a guard.

Over the winter weeks, Khan had suffered at the hands of sickness. He could barely remember what he had experienced in the town of *Bragdan*. His wounds from the dragon had finally healed and scarred over. It made Khan look like he was a battle-worn soldier.

Since the incident in the town, Khan had been able to speak to the dragon. She was quite amazing. Even though she was a little hot-headed, she was gentle with him. It took some time, but he finally figured out that her name was Cordelia. The gentle rasp of her voice calmed Khan, especially when the sickness had taken its toll on him.

Khan stopped and looked at himself as he passed a small clear puddle. His eyes were dark and puffy, his color was a pasty white.

They had been traveling for two days. Alvis was taking Khan to a cave, though he didn't know why. He sighed when the older man sped up into a jog. Khan followed but not before he let out a bout of coughing fits. His attention was driven to a familiar sound of wings beating the air just above the top of the trees.

"Tell your dragon to keep out of sight. People 'round here don't care for them like you do." Said Alvis over his shoulder.

Khan shook his head. How exactly was he supposed to do that? He furrowed his brow and opened his mouth but quickly shut it when Cordelia came gliding down to him. Her face was a mask of confusion as she landed and stared at him.

"I knew what you were thinking." Cordelia whispered as she walked beside him.

Khan didn't understand. So she could hear his thoughts? That didn't mean anything, did it? Khan gulped as Alvis stopped at a cave.

"You two must go forth into the cave and seek out the knowledge it holds." He said as he backed away from the mouth of the cave.

Should I be concerned? Thought Khan as he looked questioningly from Alvis to Cordelia. Was this really happening? Was this a dream Khan would soon wake from? He shook his head to clear his thoughts while he slowly trudged forward. Cordelia softly padded after him, her gaze shifting to Alvis as the man backed away.

As Khan and Cordelia walked down the descending path, Khan could feel a warm exhilaration in his chest. He guessed Cordelia could feel it too. She was as silent as a snowfall. Khan took in her lithe and muscular body, wondering what it must be like living in the sea. He quickly looked away as her eyes shifted to his.

"It's quite confining, actually. My Flight, my home, was strict. We could rarely go anywhere, only just barely out of our territory." Said Cordelia suddenly.

Khan studied her, his mouth open in disbelief, surely she couldn't hear his thoughts? *That's crazy!* He shook his head and looked back to the route ahead. Khan slowed his pace as she let out a whimpering trill and hung her head.

"Before I left, my best friend was... Well, she... She was killed... And I never got a chance to figure out why."

Khan felt sympathy for her. It seems even dragons have brutal ways toward each other just like humans. Suddenly, a thought occurred to him. He remembered his vision of the two dragons he saw when he had been transported into the sea.

"Cordelia. I've had visions or dreams. Many include the sea, and dragons. I had one about two dragons that raced down a slope. One was a blue color, kind of like you, the other was a deep, dark green. The blue dragon had gotten stuck in the red coral." Khan explained.

Cordelia lifted her broad head and gaped at him in disbelief.

"Th— That was me! With Bryne! But— How did you–?" Cordelia stammered as she stopped and turned to look back at him.

Khan's eyes searched hers frantically. All this time, were they always somehow connected? Another image flashed through his mind as they walked on.

"I saw a cave. It was after you got caught in the coral. It was eerie and dark. When I went inside, there was an egg in a bed of reeds." Continued Khan as they traveled down the cave's path.

"I know that cave!" Exclaimed Cordelia as she turned again and stopped right in front of him. They continued to walk down the path face to face, with Cordelia walking backward so she could see his face.

"Every drake and drakainling is scared to go in it. No one could even get past the mouth of it. There was something dreadful about that cave that made everyone fear it." She reminisced.

Khan looked past her as the tunnel split into two. It would take too much time to explore them both. They would have to choose. The left side looked more agreeable.

"Let's go this way." Said Khan, confidently turning slightly to the left and gesturing with his hand for her to follow.

Khan stopped and looked back when he heard Cordelia let out a grunt. Something stopped her in her tracks. Again, Khan urged for her to follow him. He watched with interest as she seemed to hit an invisible wall keeping her from him. Khan walked back over to her and waved to the right side. Cordelia nodded, took a few steps in, and looked expectantly at him. Khan gulped and walked after her. He cried out when he hit a hard barrier at the entrance of the tunnel. He hoped Cordelia couldn't hear how hard his heart was beating.

"Maybe we are meant to go our own way?" He whispered uncertainly to a confused Cordelia. Although she couldn't hear him, she seemed to understand what he meant. The barrier even took away their communication.

A cold gust of wind blew past Khan, making him shiver as he fumbled forward. Fear gripped his mind as a faint, eerie green light appeared at the end of the tunnel. He stopped in his tracks as voices echoed through the tunnel and bounced off the walls and into his ears. He was at the entrance of a cavern that had sleek, pale walls.

"Whoa," said Khan while he gently sat down on the floor when his vision began to turn black. A faint image took shape in front of him. Then he saw a bright, white and gold egg in a deep slumber.

"It has been waiting for you for more than a thousand years."

Whispered the eerie voice.

Khan stared at it in amazement. It's been waiting a thousand years for me?

"The King must arise, or Dragon-kind shall fall and the wings of war shall sound."

Then another image invaded his mind.

Dragons lay slaughtered on the ground, each one bloodied and broken. In horror, he helplessly watched thousands of men, in dirty armor, dying alongside the dragons. A river of fire expanded beyond the battle as it ravaged the world of life.

There was the voice again, saying,

"Now you see the consequences that will follow if the King does not arise. Both man and dragon will perish."

Khan took his head in his hands and gripped his hair between his fingers. Desperately, he tried to gather his thoughts when the images stopped. He let out a soft sob and brought his knees to his chest. Khan's breath caught in his throat when his vision went black again. Another image took shape.

A large dragon was chasing after a man. Next, there was a large cliff, and the sea expanded below it. The man was desperately running toward the cliff.

"Ask the one who knows."

Whispered the same eerie voice.

Tension engulfed Khan while he watched the man draw closer to the cliff's edge. His breath left him as the dragon launched itself toward the man.

The man reached into his cloak and drew out what looked like a white and gold egg that was about triple the size of a grapefruit. With one quick movement, he thrust the egg over the edge of the cliff and into the rolling sea below. The man ducked right before the dragon's large talons clipped his head. The dragon roared, lost its balance and fell over the side.

The image faded away before Khan could get a look at the man's face. Pulling him back to reality was an indistinguishable sound that shook the cavern, causing the moisture on the roof of the cave to drop down on his head.

His curiosity peaked when he saw a faint wisp of light travel to a gaping hole in the cavern floor. Water stretched down before him.

"Dive in, and you shall know."

The voice said.

Khan shivered and swallowed hard. He moved toward the hole and stared down into the black, deep pool.

"***Dive***" echoed off the cave walls, making him cover his ears and close his eyes. "***Dive. Dive.***"

He felt compelled to obey the words. After just a few moments in this uneasy state, Khan took a deep breath and dove head-first into the dark pool of water.

Chapter III

Old Friends

Cordelia carefully made her way through the dark water. It tasted of death every time she opened her mouth to let out a worried exhale. She wondered at how Khan was faring. Hopefully, better than she was. She wished she didn't have to swim through thick, black water. Cordelia was concerned about what she had seen. In her vision there had been a river of fire and blood spread across the land.

A voice told her that these would be the consequences if the King of Dragons did not arise. Frustrated, Cordelia did not know what *king* she was supposed to find. Somehow, this egg was connected to everything. Cordelia had to find it.

She huffed out a sigh of relief as the black water began to move away. She slithered forward into a body of crystal clear blue water. Fear coursed through her as she saw Khan struggling toward the surface, but it didn't look like he was struggling for breath. She saw a familiar dragon slithering after him. Cordelia let out a trilling cry as she waded toward them. She braced herself for a rough impact. As she neared the dragon, it opened its jaws and revealed sharp, long teeth. She trilled just before she collided with it.

Cordelia struck the dragon with all her might which forced the dragon backwards. Once she separated herself from the impact, she turned toward Khan and lowered her head so Khan could grab hold of her horns. He slid himself onto her neck just above her wing joints.

The deafening sound of rushing water couldn't suppress the sound of Khan's voice echoing in her head.

"I can breathe. This is incredible!"

Cordelia let out a blast of air into the water to show she acknowledged him. A sudden force clipped her side. Khan let out a grunt and squeezed Cordelia's neck desperately trying to stay on. She twirled in the water and twisted away. When the water stilled, a familiar face stared plainly back at her.

"Baylor." Growled Cordelia. Baylor swung his talons at her, which caused her to weave out of his way. While his talons passed, Cordelia saw an opportunity. She grabbed his wrist and pulled him toward her. She thrusted her barbed wing-tip into his left shoulder. This caused him to cry out in agony and withdraw from Cordelia and Khan.

"We need to get to the cave! They may have already found it. I saw a few dragons by the entrance." Yelled Khan in Cordelia's ears.

Cordelia nodded in acknowledgment and created a burst of bubbles to hide her escape.

Her thoughts drifted back to the King of Dragons. She remembered mentioning it to her father, Sere, and he had immediately become outraged. They must have figured it out after she mentioned it to him. Surely, Sere, her own father, wouldn't be willing to betray dragon-kind and keep the King of Dragons hidden for eternity?

She mused, if this was the case, dragon-kind would cease to exist. Surely he'd understand that? Khan and Cordelia approached the cave with caution. They had to be careful not to be seen.

Cordelia slowly stopped when she saw the Monarch and her father at the cavern's mouth. Khan lighted off her neck and came up beside her face.

“It doesn’t look like they have the egg yet.” Whispered Khan as he stared down at the imposing slope.

“What if the egg was never there?” Cordelia whispered back.

“What if all of this was just a ruse to get us to come back here? So they could kill me and you?” She continued, Khan glanced at her, his face uncertain.

“Don’t think I haven’t thought about it. This is the only thing that makes sense. I can’t explain it, but it’s like the egg wants us to find it.” Cordelia stated while she gazed back down the slope. Her breath caught in her throat as a large dragon she’d never seen before, slithered out to greet the Monarch. Feathers rippled its hide, its body lean and poised. Khan gasped beside her when he realized the same thing she thought. The dragon had no wings.

Cordelia was horrified at the sight of the dragon. Hundreds of thick scars and burns marked its shoulder blades. She grimaced. His wings had been burned off. A shuddering thought invaded her mind. She remembered her mother’s broken body when she was brought back to the ocean. Her wings had been taken. Man took them from her, possibly like they did to this dragon. Shame overwhelmed her when she realized she had now become allies with a human. She was now his servant, and he was her master.

Khan glanced at her, his eyes full of shock. Cordelia hissed under her breath, she must have directed her thoughts to him.

I’m not going to do that, Cordelia. Surely, you, of all people, or… dragons, should know that.

Cordelia shuddered, ashamed she ever thought such things of Khan. She shook her head, they *had* to get the egg, no matter what.

Khan caught her gaze, agreement shone bright in his eyes. Cordelia would have to distract them if they had any hope of recovering the egg.

Suddenly, her eyes shifted to the bag that hung across Khan's shoulders. Khan followed her gaze and let out a sharp gasp as he realized her plan. Cordelia slowly crept down to a small boulder that would be around the same size of the egg. She grasped it in her talons. Cordelia lifted it into Khan's pack while he held it open and nodded. The bag seemed to hold the weight well. Satisfied that the egg would fit, Khan reached in the bag and took the rock out and discarded it.

A loud shriek echoed across the waves as Baylor swiftly swam to meet the Monarch.

"If we're going to do this, we have to do it now." Said Cordelia, her voice shaking when the dragons began to trill in anger and glanced around.

Khan nodded and swam to the cliff's edge and hid in the crevices of it. Cordelia took a deep breath and swam through the water to the edge of the slope. The dragons began to fan out and search, Baylor must have told them she was back.

Cordelia inhaled deeply and mustered up her courage. She took the breath deep from her belly. She could make out Khan's face peeking out of his hiding place and glancing at her. With her heart full of anger and spirit, Cordelia opened her mouth and commanded the ocean to obey. The ocean fell silent as she let out the loudest, ear-piercing roar she could muster. The dragons below shrieked, covered their ears and grasped their heads. She held it out for as long as she could, but the roar slowly began to die out. As it silenced, every head turned to Cordelia. Every eye glittered with confusion and rage.

The Monarch let out a shuddering roar, signaling the dragons to advance.

Cordelia watched as the wingless dragon's eyes connected with hers. She blinked, the dragon disappeared, and only when she blinked once more, it reappeared close to her. She gasped and swiftly glided backward to stifle his advance. How could a dragon do such a thing? She let out a cry of fear as the Monarch and his soldiers came above the bend. In response, Cordelia flicked her tail and swam off as fast as she could. She prayed Khan would get to that egg soon.

Cordelia was on high alert as she slid unseen into a hidden cave that only she and Bryne knew about. Kelp hid the entrance. Bryne and Cordelia had stumbled upon it during one of their 'expeditions.' She suppressed a thought of sadness at the remembrance of the young Drakaina who was now gone and now a part of the sea. Cordelia shivered as the shadows of dragons crept by the kelp covered entrance. Memories flashed through her head. The seconds ticked by. She barely noticed the stray drake that wandered into the hidden cave.

Moving quickly, Cordelia let out a silent hiss and slammed the drake into the cave wall. He hit the wall with a sickening crack. As Cordelia slowly inched out of the kelp, her heart quickened when she saw some old friends, a pod of whales, heading toward the direction Khan had taken to get to the cave.

Cordelia slowly and patiently swam beside the large, majestic whales. Their whale songs warmed her aching heart. She knew these whales by name, and each one knew her. She felt relief as no dragon seemed to be anywhere close to the cavern. Cordelia trilled a song of thanks to the whales and couldn't resist a smile as they sang back. Her heart quickened as she slowly entered the cave. No light seeped through the large mouth of the cave, it was utter darkness.

The water grew colder and colder, until it felt like ice. Cordelia gasped when she saw a small golden egg's reflection in the water. She mustered up her courage and swam up to the surface where the water had stopped. There wasn't much room in the cave, but the top rose and rose. Cordelia stared at the golden egg that was sitting in a bed of coral and reeds. Fear began to overwhelm her. What had happened to Khan? Where was he? She figured he would have made it this far. She stared at the egg. Something about it was pulling her in. As she grew closer, the egg began to pulsate with a rhythmic beat and light, illuminating the cave and everything in it. Her heart seemed to beat along with it.

Cordelia looked around. The caves had writings and paintings along the walls and ceiling. There was a big golden symbol of a swirling dragon. An egg came after it, the same egg that laid here in this cave. Two handprints were on either side of the egg. The next scene on the cave wall depicted the hatching of the egg with a small, white hatchling looking out of the shell of the egg. Cordelia didn't stay to look at the rest of the drawings.

Before grasping the egg in her claws, a loud, frustrated roar echoed off the cave walls. Cordelia's heart began to throb in her chest. She pulled the egg close to her body and flew out of the cave.

❄❄❄

She knew it was Baylor, he had found her. A few minutes after she cleared the cave entrance, Baylor had caught up with her. She managed to get enough separation from him to clearly breach the surface of the water and put a measurable distance between her and Baylor. Now, safely out of the water and in the air, she looked down, Baylor was again closing the distance between them. Another look to her flank and there he was, close enough to belch out a cloud of mist and crystals. Cordelia lost her balance as she felt the mist attach itself around the tip of her tail weighing it down. She had to find cover. She braced herself and dove through the trees. Cordelia swiftly dodged each thin sapling and maneuvered expertly. Baylor furiously roared behind her as he tried to navigate his way among the trees. Cordelia stealthily changed gears and glided around the tree area, keeping her distance from Baylor. She needed to change the momentum and go on offense.

Switching directions, she turned toward Baylor and opened her mouth wide. Everything fell silent as she let the boiling water free. The hot substance that she spewed was the consistency of hot gel, which coated and stuck to the scales of her pursuer. She would not stick around; she knew what was coming. Cordelia took off in a blaze of fury and felt a pang of regret when she heard Baylor's pitiful cries. She knew all too well the damage this would do. After all, he had once been her childhood friend.

Cordelia flew as far from Baylor as she could. She only stopped when she could no longer hear his screams.

The scent of human blood on the night wind stopped Cordelia in her tracks. She came across a small pool of blood at the top of the cliff, it smelled of Khan. She softly set the golden egg down, which she had been carrying all this time, and sat in front of the dark pool, allowing sadness to take over. She silenced her mournful cries as white flakes began to descend from the twilight sky. Cordelia gazed at them in wonder. What was this that fell from the heavens?

"It's snowing." Said a voice from behind her.

Startled, Cordelia turned toward the voice and let out a bellow of relief as she saw Khan slowly making his way up to her. His elbow was injured and still bleeding.

"A shark caught up with me before I entered the cave." Explained Khan, noticing her concern.

Cordelia was overjoyed that Khan was still alive and that the egg was safe. She watched him as he held his hand out and let the 'snow' fall into his palm.

"I've never seen this '*snow*' before." She said, collecting the egg and settling down beside Khan. He was still standing but decided to follow suit. He used her weight to steady himself and sat down next to her.

"It's kind of like really thin ice." He replied to her questioning glance.

Khan seemed to know so much about the world of men. She felt sanctuary as Khan laid the back of his head on her shoulder so he could gaze up at the darkening sky. Cordelia sighed, lowering her head on her hands in peace. She felt safe, content with Khan. Like he was the only reason she had for existing above the water.

"So, what do we do with this?" Asked Khan as he pointed at the egg Cordelia held in her arm. "Let's decide in the morning." Yawned Cordelia.

She felt Khan nod in agreement as she closed her eyes and shifted her wing over him. She snuck a peek at him and watched as he snuggled up close to her belly since it gave off the most heat. Cordelia slowly slid the egg toward him. Khan struggled to keep his teeth from chattering and grabbed the egg and cuddled back up to the warmth of her belly. *I wish I could do more.* She thought before they both drifted off to a much needed sleep.

Chapter IV

The Truth Lies with Pigs

Drea stared out to the trees as Lukas stormed away from her. The recent events that had just transpired caused a rift in Drea's and Lukas's relationship. Less than three days ago, Drea had made Damion take her out of the abandoned fish parlor where they had taken shelter in town. The ship they were traveling in had been blown to pieces by an assassin of the Wolfed Guild. She felt cooped up and just needed some fresh air. Even though it was against Lukas's better judgment, he let them go. Damion had been badly injured by an attack in town from which they narrowly escaped with their lives. It was still touch and go with Damion.

Lukas blamed Drea. She knew deep down this was her fault.

They had taken refuge with a family just outside town in a rustic cabin after fleeing the altercation in town. Damion was hurt badly and they needed help.

Drea turned her face up toward the brooding sky and let the delicate flakes wash over her face as the snow began to fall once more. She never really appreciated snow, but she believed it told a story. However, she wasn't quite sure what that story was. Drea turned back toward the cabin and went inside. She headed up the steps to the first floor of the large cabin that they were staying in. She saw Damion still sleeping in his bed. She sighed, he'd been asleep since the accident. She wondered if he'd ever wake up. Her heart hardened for a moment. She had no reason to care for the man. All he did was aggravate her. She scolded herself. He had helped her, after all.

She took a deep breath and walked back down to the kitchen.

"How you feel?" Inquired Bronwyn, with two mugs of tea in her hands.

Bronwyn was their host. She was no longer a young woman but she held her age well. At a glance, Drea could tell that she wasn't from this country. She was short, very tan and beautiful. Drea guessed she was from the Southern regions of the Dead Lands. How anyone could survive out there, Drea didn't know.

She smiled and took the mug she held in her left hand.

"Very well, thank you. The, uh, the poultice you made for my thigh is quite soothing. It stings a bit, but that's a part of the process of healing, I suppose." Said Drea as she took a sip of sweet, flowery tea.

After they finished their tea, Bronwyn washed the cups and put them away. She turned toward Drea and looked at her as if she owed her something. Drea had promised that once she felt better, she'd let Bronwyn take her to see her prize piglets. Why they were prized, Drea hadn't the faintest idea. If the truth were told, she really didn't care to know. Drea followed as Bronwyn proceeded down the narrow path to a small, wooden shack that scarcely resembled a barn.

"They this way." she pointed.

Drea coughed out a laugh; the way Bronwyn spoke played to Drea's curiosity. As they drew nearer, snorting sounds filled the air. Drea could see to one side of the shack a row of tumbling hills and a quaint town lying on the horizon. Bronwyn let out a sigh when she spotted Drea's attention toward the town. The old woman gave a gentle, understanding smile then patted at the top of Drea's hand with her own.

"You wanna run, then? Runnin' lead to more, more problem."

Drea gazed at her, unable to keep her eyes from welling with tears. She did want to run, to run far away from everything she's faced and everything that she fears will come.

"I've never felt so scared." Choked Drea as Bronwyn took hold of both her hands in sympathy.

"Fear of runnin' away? Fear of losin'? Fear of yous' self? Fear not haf' to define us. We haf' to define fear." Said Bronwyn as she pulled Drea into the shack.

Drea shuddered, she didn't know what she was afraid of, or who. She sniffed and instantly regretted it, covering her nose and mouth swiftly with one hand. Bronwyn let out a light burst of laughter.

"It smell bad, no?"

Drea looked at her for a moment in silence before bursting out into a bout of laughter too.

Bronwyn smiled as the piglets rolled around in the mucky, and very oddly smelling, dark mud. Drea squatted and began patting the piglets. Bronwyn's eyes sparkled in pride and for whatever reason, this made Drea happy.

❄❄❄

The sound of birds chirping and the faint crackle of an ongoing fire awoke Drea from her peaceful sleep. She looked around the room. Damion's bed was empty, the sheets tucked neatly into the sides. Drea sat up in her bed with a stretch and a yawn.

"Oh, finally, you're awake. Come on and eat." Said a voice at the entrance of the room.

Drea looked up to see Damion leaning on the door casing, staring at her. Drea chewed the inside of her cheek as she looked away. *Great. Goodbye peace and quiet.* She thought before she pulled her covers off. The room was cold, and the floor was even colder as her feet touched the ground. Right then, something landed on her head. Damion had thrown a thick, knitted sweater at her. Pulling it off her head, she gave him an angry look. Then, she quickly slipped her head and arms into the warm sweater and stood up. She groaned and followed after him. Looking at him made Drea feel bad. Damion had a horribly bruised cheek and a swollen, black eye. Not to mention the other injuries that he had suffered from the soldiers they met at the market a few days ago.

He seemed to smile no matter what life seemed to throw at him. Maybe that's what Drea loathed the most, well, his attitude was definitely a close second. She shook her head to clear her thoughts and pulled out her seat at the table to sit next to Bronwyn. Bronwyn smiled sweetly at her before turning her attention back to her meal.

As Drea waited for her breakfast, the palm of her right hand started to ache and sent twinges down to the tips of her fingers. She began to rub the palm of her hand and slowly her vision darkened and an image slowly appeared in her mind's eye.

She saw Khan, but it wasn't Khan, it couldn't be. He rode on the back of a bright, lithe, blue dragon as it soared above the clouds. Khan pulled something out of his satchel. Then….

The image was disrupted as Damion set a plate of food down in front of her. She groaned inwardly as he pulled up a chair beside her.

“Not all awake, are we?” Said Damion as he sat down in his chair.

Drea resisted the urge to pull every fine hair from his head and leave him bald. She bit her tongue, and decided to play nice for once.

Drea balled her hands into fists but winced when her hand pulsed with a bout of pain. She rubbed it gently. Damion continued to try to make light conversation with her. Lukas shot her a warning glare causing her to take up Damion’s conversation with a forced smile. Drea’s eyes dropped to her plate. She pushed around its contents with her fork and slouched back against her chair. She struggled to swallow the large lump in her throat. It seemed Lukas was still angry with her, but of what instance she was unsure. Was it about her attempted assassination of Lord Ragnar? Or her betrayal of him and Khan? Or the recent altercation in town that left Damion badly injured? She figured it was all the above. She hung her head and started eating.

❄❄❄

“Hey! Drea! Ouch! Come on, wait!” Said Damion as he followed after her.

Drea tried to ignore him with all her might as she tugged along a small, fluffy fir tree. They had been sent out together to gather firewood. Drea had tried to talk her way out of it, but Lukas was too stubborn.

“What’d I do to make you hate me?” Asked Damion, his voice beginning to sound sorrowful.

Drea stopped in her tracks and looked up into the trees. *Why must he make this difficult?* Drea didn't exactly know how to answer that question. She clenched her jaw shut. She turned and instantly felt regret when she saw his face contorted with pain as he struggled to keep his footing. Damion wasn’t fully recovered from his injuries and he tried to carry more firewood than he should have. Drea glanced at his legs, he was favoring his right foot. He had a heavy bag laid on his shoulder that he kept a tight hold on with one hand. Damion clung to a tree almost twice the size of hers trying to drag it along. As he tried to move forward, his left knee gave way and he tumbled to the forest floor. Drea swiftly sprinted over to him to shove the heavy sack of wood off his back and help him sit up. Drea looked at him in pity. Surely, his injuries should have healed by now. His left knee did look swollen, she thought. Drea stood straight and held out her hand to help him up. After he was up and steady, Drea heard a distant sound in the trees. Something felt very wrong with this place. The look of alarm on her face caused Damion to look around.

"What?" He said, trying to understand what was happening.

When the feeling was gone, Drea shook her head and looked back to him.

Damion gave her a look she wasn't used to, which made her a bit uncomfortable. Turning away, Drea bent over, grabbed his heavy sack of wood and swung it over her shoulders before reaching down to grab the stump of Damion's tree. Damion limped after her in surprise.

"Uh, can I help with that?" He said, breaking the awkward silence.

Drea stopped walking and turned toward him, then glanced at her small tree. Her tree was meant to be decorated for the winter season. Not too big and not too small. The big tree was for firewood.

"Uh, n---no, but... Really?"

Drea glanced back at him and nodded her head ruefully. Damion clenched his teeth and sighed as he took hold of the tree in anger.

“Can’t I just...” Damion started,

“No, you are in no condition to be pulling this much weight.” Drea said, cutting him off mid-sentence.

Damion came up beside her at the foot of a hill and side-eyed her. Drea groaned, and said, “Fine, but just this time.”

He let out a triumphant laugh and took his tree back out of her grip. Drea flinched away from his palm as it pressed down on her hand. Her hand throbbed with pain and she didn't know why. She thought maybe from the weight of the tree or the sudden movement of Damion pulling the tree out of her hand. He looked at her, confusion on his face. Drea looked down at her hand, then instantly hid it and grabbed the other end of the tree. It had been feeling weird all morning.

❄❄❄

“Fine tree!” Said Lukas, helping Damion pull his tree up the front porch steps and into the house.

Drea walked inside, dropped the sack of wood by the door and pushed the door shut with her heel. Several thoughts were roaming through her mind as she slid off her boots and took off her jacket and scarf. Something was wrong here, everything felt out of place. She went upstairs and slowly pushed open the door to the room she was staying in, walked blindly to her bed and plopped down hard.

Why was she important to the King? Why did he want her dead? Why did he need to chase her around the kingdoms just to end an insignificant orphan’s life? None of it made sense. The fire in the room crackled softly. Drea laid her head down on the fluffed pillow and stared up at the ceiling. The warmth of the fire began to spread around the room. Drea turned on her side and faced away from the door. Exhaustion began to take over and she struggled to keep her eyes open.

"You're in my bed." Said Damion's voice at the door.

Almost asleep, she jumped at his voice. She got out of the bed and apologized, realizing her bed was the next one over. A few moments after Drea settled underneath her covers, a voice sounded at the door again. Drea sighed and closed her eyes, it was too low for her to hear. She sighed and kept her eyes shut as Damion's footsteps came toward her.

She resisted a smile as she felt him spread a thick, warm quilt across her. Sleep overwhelmed her as Damion's footsteps receded.

Chapter V

White Bridge

Khan sighed with accomplishment as he held the egg in his hands. Cordelia looked protectively at it.

It had been several days since they had retrieved the egg. They weren't exactly sure how to take care of it. They argued about where to keep the egg. They both made suggestions and both rationalized why the other's idea was bad. Eventually, they decided the best way to keep it safe would be for them to take it with them wherever they went. Khan opened his pack and gently laid the egg inside while Cordelia bent down, allowing Khan to climb onto her shoulders. There was one place they could go, but Khan didn't know exactly how to get there.

"Cordelia, do you think you could find the White Bridge Kingdom? The castle itself?" Asked Khan as Cordelia glided up toward the clouds.

"Maybe. I have passed a few large buildings with pointed roofs. Is that a castle?"

"Yes. It's in the Shauburns Wood, I think." Said Khan as he studied the forest below. He regretted that he hadn't always paid attention to the elders' teachings.

"Where's that?" Asked Cordelia, her head swinging around to look at him.

Khan thought for a moment, he never really knew where every kingdom was. He sighed, they would have to ask someone. Cordelia heard his thoughts. She acknowledged him with a flicker of her ear.

"Stop at the..." Started Khan as a thought occurred to him.

"Can you go back to where the cave was?" He asked. Cordelia looked back at him, her brow furrowed as she tried to remember.

After a moment, she agilely changed directions. This quick movement almost made Khan slip off Cordelia's shoulders. She trilled an apology, easing her speed to allow him to reset himself and get a better hold. The height they were at scared him. Trying not to look down, Khan kept his gaze forward as Cordelia climbed even higher and gained more and more speed.

❄❄❄

They arrived back at Alvis's home after a few hours of searching for the castle unsuccessfully. Khan followed Alvis to a back room that served as a crude office where he showed him an old, tattered map. Before Khan could get a proper look, the old man swiftly rolled it up and shoved it into an extra bag that held some bread, a few apples, and a canteen full of water. The old man pulled Khan into a tight hug and patted his back roughly.

"Go swiftly. Soldiers from the Durklin Kingdom are ransacking homes nearby and looking for the one who rides the flying beast." He said with concern in his voice.

Khan pulled away and looked at Alvis, he furrowed his brow as he saw a glimpse of fear spread through the old man's eyes. Slowly, Khan nodded and walked out of the house. He looked back at the open door where Alvis and Elina stood, waving him off.

"Get to White Bridge as quickly as you can!" Shouted Alvis. Determined, Khan pulled himself up on the spare horse Alvis had in his barn, its large hooves sliding in the snow with each step. It was a better choice than having Cordelia be seen and shot down with Khan astride. The best thing was for her to stay hidden for as long as possible. Khan decided that he and Cordelia would split up and go different ways. Cordelia was unhappy with Khan's plan but agreed to do what he asked. Khan would head east while Cordelia would head south for a while, and then turn back toward the east, so they could meet up at the White Kingdom.

But before he could glance at the map, the pounding of hooves hitting the ground sounded down the trail. Khan glanced at Alvis, who forced his wife back inside and yelled at Khan to go. Khan groaned as he dug his heels into the horse's side. It let out a swift whinny and charged forward.

❄❄❄

Khan held tight to the reins and tugged gently on them to slow his horse as they made it to the top of the mountain ridge. Rage, sadness, and fear stabbed his heart all at once as he saw the forest where Alvis and his family lived going up in flames behind him. He fought to keep his composure. Surely, the Great King Dolion wasn't going to kill anyone associated with Khan and Drea? What did Khan and his sister do to make the King so ruthless to his own people? Sure, he ruled over all of the nine kingdoms, but killing people would just make his people angry and rebel.

A thought echoed in his mind as the wind began to pick up and several drops of rain fell on Khan's face. He was pulled back to reality by the sound of hounds barking not too far behind him. With urgency, Khan kicked his horse to put distance between him and his pursuers.

❄❄❄

Khan urged his horse to its top speed as arrows whizzed through the air just above his head. "Come on, just a little farther." he encouraged his horse. There was a curve up ahead that led to a small town called *Icemeet.* After that, it would be straight on to the White Bridge Kingdom for another three hours.

Khan screamed and suddenly rocketed forward, over the neck of his horse. He groaned in pain as he hit his back painfully on a fallen tree that snapped under his weight. After the shock of the impact, Khan looked around and saw his horse struggling to stand after its front right leg was caught in a rabbit hole. He watched in agony as an arrow swiftly hit the horse on the side of its head. Khan stood and took hold of his satchel and bolted toward the town road. He ran as fast as he could, despite his twisted ankle that he had suffered from the impact of the fall. Khan shouted and roared at the people to move and get out of the way as he pushed through the crowd. Everyone screamed as a loud crack went out and the smell of smoke hit Khan's nose.

"Everyone on your knees!" Bellowed a deep and booming voice.

Instantly, everyone dropped to their knees. Khan swiftly followed and kept his face hidden.

Who were these men? They didn't look like soldiers from a Kingdom, they were too unkept and cruel. Every man but the leader wore the Kingdom's colors. Although these colors were not of a Kingdom he knew of. To be fair, the Durklin Kingdom, which he assumed these men were from, was full of barbarians, bounty hunters and drunkards. The crowd screamed, while the men pushed their way through, searching for someone. Khan held his breath. Two men stopped a foot from him, their eyes searching the mob of faces. The next thing he knew, a hand reached down and gripped his hair, hoisting him up. Khan fought, the grip got tighter as he was pulled from the crowd. The man loosened his grip and shoved Khan in the back, causing him to stumble forward. Before he hit the ground, he threw out his arms to soften his fall.

"Where's your other half?" Said a voice above him.

Khan swiftly took a knee and looked up at the man in front of him. He was astride a monstrous bay stallion. It had a helmet across its face with sharp points. Khan glared at him confused, making the man repeat the question. Was he talking about Drea? Or Cordelia?

"I don't know what you're talking about." Said Khan casually. Hopefully, there was a way he could talk his way out of this.

The man shook his head in disappointment and dismounted his horse. Khan stood defiantly. The man stepped toward him, letting out a sly but dangerous chuckle as he tapped the large hilt of his sheathed sword. Khan gulped, this man was almost a full head taller than him.

"Don't play with me boy, there's a lot more at stake if you don't communicate." The man boomed.

Khan followed his gaze and took a step back. What lord would let his men murder an entire village of innocent victims? His own village at that.

"Those who even look at you are guilty of treason." Said the man as he circled Khan, "I didn't even..." "Ah, ah, ah. Make an argument or even think of stepping to me. We'll burn this village to the ground with you in it." Hissed the man in Khan's ear.

Khan racked his brain. What was he supposed to do? He didn't do anything to anger these men or the King that he was aware of.

"I heard you acquired something belonging to the King. Give it to me, and come with us and we will let everyone go." demanded the man.

Khan glared at him, considering the options. Would he really give his life and the egg to people he didn't know? Suddenly, Khan furrowed his brow, how did they know about the egg?

The man smiled as he noticed Khan's confusion and said, "We have our resources."

Khan sighed and handed over his satchels and followed the man to a small horse. They knew they were going to capture him. He looked back at the crowd of people still glancing around frantically in fear as they knelt in submission.

"You'll leave them be?" Asked Khan as he pulled himself onto the horse.

The man shook his head and looked at Khan with a false look of innocence in his eyes that flashed with a hunger for blood. Behind the hunger, there was something else Khan couldn't place when the man looked back to the village.

"No!" Khan yelled.

The men began to set homes on fire and they laughed with pleasure. The man didn't seem to share his soldiers' delight.

Anger, fear, and hate consumed Khan's thoughts. At that moment, lightning cracked which made Khan's horse rear and snort. As the horse's hooves hit the ground, rain began pouring down and put out the fires. The crowd shrieked, roots and branches shot out of the ground and took the foul men off their feet and into the air. Khan's eyes and head felt like they were on fire. He rolled down from his horse. Khan yelled in pain, causing an earth-shattering roar to split through the rumbling thunder.

Ever so slowly, the rain began to ease off, allowing the sun to shine through. Khan looked up and saw a well-dressed woman with short swords fastened on both of her hips. There was a large, broad, muscular dragon standing tall behind her. Its breath came out in short bursts of mist. Khan crawled backward and a hand clasped at his shoulder. The man who tried to capture Khan, was struggling to get to his feet and groaned in pain. Khan stood with him and glared defiantly at him. At first, Khan only noticed a trace of blood coming from the man's mouth. With a closer look, he noticed a thick, sharp branch embedded in his shoulder.

"My Lady Helene." He said as he struggled up onto his horse.

Khan studied the woman by the dragon. He gasped, it was her. Khan had found the White Bridge Kingdom.

"Good to see you, my friend, if only it were under different circumstances." Said Lady Helene to the man with a gentle edge on her voice.

"Do not come here again and threaten my people unless you want to lose your head, Durlak." Warned Lady Helene, her right hand resting on the hilt of one of her swords.

The man nodded in submission, kicked his horse into a fast trot and headed away from the town with the rest of his thugs.

Khan watched the Lady with interest. What if she didn't accept him? Would she turn him away? She walked over to him and laid her hand on his shoulder. She gestured her head to her dragon and said, "Come." They both mounted the great beast, and with a click of her mouth, Lady Helene raised the rein, pulling the dragon's head upward and allowing it to lift itself up into the air.

❄❄❄

After what seemed like a two hour long ride, Khan was overwhelmed and exhausted. He looked down, they had covered a lot of ground quickly. Down below them was the White Bridge. He had never seen it from this vantage point before. He held gently to Lady Helene's waist as they glided back to her castle. Khan's happiness slowly disappeared as he remembered Drea. Several memories flashed through his head. When she first rode Rán, when they met Lukas and Gael, when Khan almost lost her.

What if he has lost her? What if he died before he saw her again? Lady Helene asked him if he was alright after she felt his grip loosen.

He lied and said, "I'm fine." then looked down to the path below. How much farther would Khan have to run to be safe? Khan wondered where Cordelia was and if she was okay.

Khan's thoughts were suddenly brought back to the man who had come after him and chased him into that small village. Durlak, she called him, had something of his. He had Khan's bag.

Khan looked in amazement as Lady Helene's dragon circled a city stationed on an island connected to the rest of the world by a gleaming white bridge.

Chapter VI

The Cold-Dwellers

Cordelia glided inches above the turquoise waves. Every now and then, a friendly dolphin would jump out and swim beside her. She felt rejuvenated whenever she was near water but tired when she was far from it. The thought of the wingless dragon who suddenly appeared close to her when it had been a great distance away troubled her greatly. She had never seen such a thing, or such a dragon. The fact that there were so many things unknown to Cordelia was indeed troubling which caused her to doubt what she was really here for. Khan slowly entered her mind as she let the waves engulf her legs and arms. Was he alright? Did he make it to the White Bridge?

She pulled away from the waves as she felt Khan's extra satchel being tugged on her shoulder. Gliding slowly toward a steep cliff, Cordelia chose a safe spot and landed gently on a piece of rock that jutted out from the cliff's rocky face. She let out a contented sigh and opened the satchel to reveal the golden egg. Cordelia felt a new sense of responsibility for her new charge. It gave her another reason to not swim away, but to stay and help Khan fight whatever battle he was forced to fight.

Cordelia turned to the sea, feeling her scales rise as though she was being watched. She carefully shut the bag, jumped off the rock and launched back into the air. She flew away from the cliff and spotted another patch of land a little way off and headed in that direction. Cordelia finally arrived at the small patch of land. She beat her wings a few times to slow her descent. She landed with a gentle thud beside a tree that she plopped down against in exhaustion.

❄❄❄

Cordelia woke with a sense of awareness. She raised her head to a swift call that sounded in the darkness. Her ears caught the sound of footsteps. Her breath caught in her throat. She didn't recognize them as Khan's. She tightened her grip on the satchel that held the egg as the call sounded again but, this time closer. Her chest rumbled with a growl. She watched a shadow that looked like a human circle around her. Not too close to see who it was, but not too far to not be able to see anything.

Eerie whispers floated in the air as yellow and green lights flashed here and there. Snow began to fall once more and she couldn't help but shiver from a frigid wind that blew past her. Cordelia's chest tightened. There was a shadow of something approaching. It wasn't the human's shadow. Cordelia stood while bowing her head and pulled the satchel string around her neck. She didn't feel welcome here. As she spread her wings, a multitude of voices, deep and high, uttered in unison behind her, "Don't leave. We're not finished with you yet."

Cordelia gulped and turned back. She almost had to close her eyes as she faced a horrifying creature. Something was very wrong here. It shrieked at her, baring its sharp, long teeth. Cordelia backed away as it took several steps toward her.

Though Cordelia was double its size, she couldn't help but feel fear as one after the other appeared. She let out a roar of pain as something sharp grabbed her ankle. She swiftly turned, took hold of whatever it was and bit down with all her might. She flinched at the sickening crunch and the odd taste of something unknown. Cordelia dropped the corpse triumphantly. It swiftly vanished into a pile of ashes. The remaining creatures began to hiss and let out guttural sounds as they advanced on her. She cried out as she felt two more bites along her tail. Cordelia grabbed the closest one and swung it with all her might. The creatures let out wavering shrieks as they flew through the air. She roared, taking off from the ground but was instantly overwhelmed by the creatures who launched themselves atop her.

She trilled in pain and finally she landed painfully with a loud thump. Cordelia felt helpless while the creatures clawed and bit at her flesh. Falling limp she felt something set in her veins. Her limbs went stiff and Cordelia could no longer move. She closed her eyes and let out one final trill of anguish. She felt her scales being pulled off one by one. She was slowly being eaten alive.

Cordelia's eyes flashed open to the sound of a loud earth-shattering roar above her. The creatures shrieked as they were being pulled off Cordelia in rapid succession. Out of the corner of her eye, she could see large creatures battling the smaller band of creatures with great strength.

"Get her out of here!" Shrieked one of the larger creatures, a rough rasp to its voice.

She gasped and pulled away as the face of a creature she couldn't identify, moved up to inspect her.

"She's been bit!" It shrieked,

"Then carry her! Get her out!"

Cordelia groaned as she was pulled up to its large shoulders and carted away. She jerked every time the creature set its feet on the ground. She felt sick, the venom was excruciating; it made her vision and limbs dull and numb.

Cordelia felt herself leaving the ground and being launched into the air.

She felt herself slipping and falling, unable to spread her wings. In a single moment, talons wrapped around her shoulders and waist. One of the creatures caught her midair. While aloft in the air, the moon shone brightly and allowed Cordelia to see the outline of her savior. She could make out a large head, multiple horns rising from its skull, and tendrils acting as whiskers. Above the rushing sound of wind, Cordelia could hear the faint beat of wings. She shuddered and a moan escaped her throat. She felt the creature's snout touch her ear and whisper to her, "You'll be okay." And Cordelia gave in to unconsciousness.

❄❄❄

Cordelia woke up with a start. She almost choked when water slipped into her lungs. Slowly, she propped herself up from her surprisingly comfortable reed bed and scanned the area. She could barely see; it must be night still. On the opposite side of the den, she noticed a creature sleeping soundly. Cordelia slowly crept to the mouth of the den and stopped immediately at the sound of a gentle voice saying, "It's late, you won't be able to see soon. Stay and rest."

Cordelia sighed and turned back to the creature. It stared at her with gentle, intelligent eyes. Suddenly, it grinned and looked away as it mumbled, "You think I'm intelligent?"

Cordelia couldn't believe it, did it know what she was thinking?

Slowly, the creature let out a fume of sizzling light from its mouth and slithered out of its bed of reeds. The light fizzed inside a water bubble. Before its mouth closed, Cordelia could see streaks of light that looked a little bit like lightning flashing around the creature's teeth.

She gazed at the light; how was it possible for light like this to be in water? Cordelia slithered away from the creature as it floated slowly toward her.

"I'm not a creature." It said, a sad twang in its words, "I'm like you."

Cordelia still continued to back away even when the creature's face was illuminated by the light. It was right, it was her kin; it was a Sea dragon. Cordelia wasn't sure what type, she didn't even know other Sea dragons existed outside her Flight.

The dragon was a pale purple and white; its white scales shimmered with gold edges. The light caught it as it shifted every now and then, its eyes were a gentle pink. He looked much older than her, at least close to becoming an adult, maybe? It nodded and waved its tail, pointing to a reed bed holding a wrapped up blue-green egg.

"Its mother passed not too long ago." Said the dragon, sorrow clinging to his words. "My name is Atlas."

Cordelia looked at him with sympathy; she knew what it was like. She had no mother growing up, now, she was pretty sure she didn't have a father anymore either.

"I'm sorry." Whispered the dragon as he still gazed at his egg.

Cordelia shifted awkwardly, she didn't like someone reading her thoughts. Cordelia couldn't help but feel relieved as the dragon looked away ashamed. She spotted the egg that she and Khan had rescued in another reed bed, following him as he slowly swam out of the cave and into the open depths.

"Where one thing ends, another begins." Said the dragon while he overlooked the coral coves and reeds.

Cordelia glanced at him, unsure what he meant. The dragon side-eyed her, he shook his head and turned back to the cave. Cordelia stared after him, what did that mean, she wondered.

She ran the saying repeatedly in her head, *Where one thing ends, another begins*. She still couldn't understand.

"Maybe you aren't meant to know, yet." Said the dragon from inside the cave.

Cordelia looked toward the surface, wondering if she should take flight and leave, or stay. Too many thoughts rippled through her head, she could not get a clear one. She hung her head and slithered back to the cave.

❄❄❄

Cordelia and Atlas swam near a pod of whales; each whale vocalized with their own, unique song. Several days had passed, Cordelia was now sure she could trust Atlas with her secrets.

Though, he may have already known them.

Atlas had become sort of like a brother, a friend Cordelia could go to, but it still wasn't exactly the same. Cordelia slowly swam to a halt.

An image of Bryne slowly fluttered into Cordelia's mind. The thought of her long-lost friend made Cordelia want to weep. Baylor had viciously taken her life for a reason Cordelia was yet to figure out. Perhaps, it was Bryne who betrayed them, and Baylor took her life in defense to protect himself? Cordelia shuddered as a voice sang in the back of her head.

"In the arms of a friend, one must bear the other's weight."

Cordelia was brought back to reality as Atlas swam back to her and sent a band of bubbles at her from stopping so quickly. She took a breath in and held it; she figured it was time.

Chapter VII

Falling Out

Days bled into weeks and weeks slowly bled into a month. For Drea, it seemed as if she had lived thirty lifetimes. She didn't like hiding, and she didn't like fighting either. *It all would end up being worthless,* she thought. Drea, Lukas, and Damion had left Bronwyn's home after Damion was healthy enough to go.

When they were halfway from the town, Bronwyn's home was set ablaze on a snowy night. Bronwyn and her whole family suffered a tragic death because of them. Drea was devastated. Now, once again, the trio was on the run. The King's soldiers closed in at every turn. Drea didn't exactly know where she was.

Khan and the others from the ship Leona were nowhere to be found. The saddest part was that her faithful dog, Gael was also missing. Drea hoped she was alive and faring well. Drea's and Lukas's relationship had become heated. It felt like they could never stop fighting. Poor Damion had to listen to the constant bickering and had to break up arguments before they turned to fights. Drea was in a war she would never understand. Every part of her wanted to give up and leave Damion and Lukas to fend for themselves. The other part of her wanted to spare them from the grief she carried; she knew it showed, unintentionally.

She swallowed down the lump that floated in her throat before emotion could show. Trying to shake off her melancholy thoughts, she gathered her wits and gently kicked Damion awake. He woke with a start and gazed tiredly up at Drea.

"What?" Asked Damion, his words slurred as he struggled to stay awake.

"It's your watch now." Whispered Drea taking Damion's quilt once he pulled it off and sat up. Damion let out a groan and rubbed his hands together to get warm. Drea shook her head at him and helped him up from the uneven earth. His stomach growled harshly and they were reminded of winter's toll.

Drea sighed and settled down in Damion's slightly warm sleeping space. She hoped the snow would soon stop and allow them some peace. Why did it have to be so cold? She tried to settle down and sleep, but her mind just wouldn't shut down. She kept thinking about King Dolion, and what she and Khan could have possibly done to anger him enough to want them dead. She inhaled sharply, a voice whispered in her ear.

"The time will come for you to understand our meaning."

She felt her anger start to rise. All these voices ever did was get her into trouble. She pushed away the voice, furrowed her brow and shut her eyes. Drea sighed, where would this take her? And what did it all mean? She swiped away a falling tear and canceled out her thoughts as sleep overtook her.

❄❄❄

"The time will come for you to understand our meaning."

Drea woke up with a start, and sitting up she took in her surroundings. Where was she? She couldn't tell if it was walls or trees in front and behind her. It was so hot, now she could see that she was in a forest and everything in it was on fire. She quickly covered her face as flames lashed at her. Distorted howls erupted around her through the fierce wind.

"Drea!" Shrieked a voice.

Drea jumped up; it was Damion. She ran toward the sound of him yelling her name. Drea skidded to a halt at the drop of a steep cliff. She glanced around left and right, Damion was nowhere to be seen. Finally when he called her name again, she spotted him. Through the smoke and the flames, Damion was searching frantically for a way out of the brush. Drea watched with fear when three pairs of red eyes appeared behind him. He couldn't see them!

"Damion!" She cried as the first creature launched itself at him.

Causing him to cry out in pain. The creature's fangs dug into his thigh. They were wolves, but what reason would they have to attack? As she watched, the other two wolves advanced and surrounded him.

"Damion!" Shrieked Drea. She watched helplessly while the three wolves knocked Damion onto the dirt.

Then, for whatever reason, the wolves pulled away. Her heart stopped. Three howls echoed into the wind as the three wolves melted into each other to create a strong-looking soldier. Damion met her gaze just as the edge of a blade came out of his stomach. The soldier held his shoulders as he fell to the ground. She let out a sob and both Damion and the soldier disappeared. She dropped to her knees in anguish and covered her face with her hands.

Then the voice whispered in her head once again.

"The time will come for you to understand our meaning."

She screamed. Her eyes burned in her head; the pain was excruciating like fire was burning away at her mind and body.

She gasped and looked up, cold air rushed past her. Lukas stood in front of her. His eyes gazed down at her, his brow furrowed. Then something large slowly came up behind him. A chill ran down her spine as a sword was thrust into his stomach from behind. Through her tears, she could vaguely make out the large face of a dragon. She could make out half of a dirty, brown skull. The cold, green eyes connected with hers, then it swung its large talons toward Lukas to deliver the final blow. What was happening to her?

"No!" She screamed as she watched these events unfold.

A clear sheet of sky rose from the smoke and shone brightly. She closed her eyes and then there it was again, the voice.

"Look, child, look and see the reason."

Drea turned her head away from where she was supposed to look. She would not give this thing, whatever it was, the satisfaction. Then louder it boomed,

"Look! Look, child!"

❄❄❄

Drea woke up with a start. Damion was shaking her awake. She pushed his hands away and gaped at him. She sucked in a long, deep breath and exhaled in relief. Thankfully, it had all been a dream. Her mind was foggy, either from the lack of sleep or from the events in her dream. Damion called her name again.

"What?" Mumbled Drea as she slowly sat up.

"There's something you should probably see." concern in his voice.

Drea groaned inwardly while she stood up, she swung her quilt over her shoulders and wrapped her arms up inside. She ignored Lukas's gaze, walked over, and looked around.

"I don't see anything." Said Drea, looking back at Damion.

She wasn't sure, but thought she saw fear flickering in his eyes. Lukas softly gripped her chin and tilted her head toward the sky. *Dragons!*

"They're letting themselves be known." Said Lukas as he glanced back to the sky.

"Surely they know the risks?" Asked Drea while she stared at the large group of dragons converging, flying just below the clouds.

Lukas said nothing, just sighed and hung his head. He could not give a rational answer for that. Drea looked away from him; her gaze shifted now to the rolling hills. She squinted, spotting something coming down the hill at a fast pace toward them.

"What is that?" Asked Damion pointing to the very place she was looking.

Lukas followed their gaze, instantly putting a hand over his brow to block out the sun. Suddenly, something blood red and black shot up from the unknown object. Fear clutched Drea's heart as several more figures came down the hill toward them.

Something twice as large as the others rose over the top of the hill. Drea stood frozen, while Lukas and Damion turned and ran. Just then a thick, glowing red ball of fire came their way.

"Drea!" Lukas yelled, clutching Drea's shoulders and bringing her back to reality.

She stumbled blindly; unsure of what to make of things. She dove forward, as the great ball of fire exploded just a few feet behind her. Lukas flew about six feet forward and his body hit the base of a large tree. Damion came rushing to Drea but she shoved him away.

"No! Help him!" She yelled and pointed toward Lukas.

Damion nodded and ran over to Lukas. Drea stood and let out a groan; her vision was shaky and her ears were ringing.

She quickly followed after Damion and took hold of Lukas's other arm. Ever so gently, they helped Lukas to stand. They could stay there no longer, it wasn't safe.

The trio picked up their pace. How did the enemy even manage to find them? They were at a disadvantage. They had no weapons that they could use to fight. Faintly, they could hear the clip-clop of horses heading toward them. They'd never be able to outrun them, especially with the type of firepower their pursuers had. There just had to be a way. There had to be. Drea frantically looked around. It couldn't end here! There! In the bracken, she could see a deep hole there.

"This way!" Cried Drea while she ran toward it.

"Drea, no! If we go in there we'll be trapped!" Said Lukas as he chased after her.

In a flurry of panic, she didn't listen to him. She ran straight for it. Just before she reached the spot, hands grabbed her shoulders and pulled her away as a bright ball of fire blasted the rock above it sealing the entrance. She turned to see Lukas holding her back. Anger flared inside of her.

"What are you doing? I could have made it!" Yelled Drea. Lukas nodded bitterly.

"Yeah. *YOU* would have made it." Growled Lukas.

Drea's anger diminished and was replaced with shame. She had been only thinking of herself.

"If I didn't stop you Drea, there was very little chance you would have made it!" Shouted Lukas throwing his hands toward the debris of rocks scattered around the entrance, including a large boulder blocking the entrance.

"We wouldn't be in this situation if we had left Bronwyn's house when I asked!" Stated Drea, her fingers balling into fists.

"No, you wanted to leave for your own pride! I know you hated it there. Just like you hated Damion!" Countered Lukas, his eyes flaring with anger while he pointed a finger toward Damion.

Damion glanced up at him with a somber face. Lukas met Damion's gaze before he looked back at Drea. This time the only look of Lukas's face was the look of apathy.

"Like you hated me." Said Lukas simply. Drea took a step back.

"But… I—" Started Drea before she was cut off by Lukas.

"None of this would have *ever* happened if you hadn't left when I told you not too!" Hissed Lukas as he pushed her a few inches away from him. Damion took a step forward.

Drea's anger rekindled.

"*I* wouldn't be in this situation if you had looked for me when I was taken!" Shrieked Drea while she shoved Lukas with both hands.

The man she once knew disappeared. He swept at her feet with his foot. Taking her by surprise, her right foot was knocked out from under her and she was caught off balance. Before she could react,

Lukas foot went into her stomach. Drea cried out as she toppled backwards and hit the ground painfully.

"Lukas!" Shouted Damion. Before Damion reached her, Lukas shoved him away and went after Drea.

She gasped while she fought off his hands. She stood quickly, only to be sent to the ground once again. Drea let out a cough and a groan when her back and head hit the ground. Before she could get a breath, Lukas's hands wrapped around her throat. In his haze of anger, he had turned on her.

Drea slapped and kicked trying to get him off. She pulled at his hands. Damion came running and launched himself into Lukas's side. The two went flying off and down a hill. Drea took gasping breaths and coughed as she finally got air. She groaned and sat up before getting all the way up. She shook her head and quickly went after the two.

❄❄❄

Drea carefully made her way down to the stream where Lukas and Damion had ended up. She glanced around, she didn't see them.

Just as she turned, Lukas launched himself at her. She ducked and rolled out of the way. As Lukas rounded on her, Damion came out of the blue and placed a well aimed punch on Lukas's jaw. Lukas fell sideways and groaned as he caught himself. His eyes met Drea's from where she hid behind a tree. Damion's foot disrupted the view.

"I did. I did look for you, Drea. Wasted a lot of time by the looks of it. Because all you became was a killer." Said Lukas as he stood. Damion's tense position slackened.

Drea came out of hiding but made sure to keep Damion between her and Lukas. Sadness crept into her heart as she accepted the heavy truth.

"You should have let Jax kill me. You should have left me on the boat." She said while she hung her head. Damion glanced back at her before turning toward her as he waited for Lukas's response.

"I should have." He answered and there seemed to be no anger, grief or guilt in his response.

Drea's heart sank while Damion looked back at Lukas with despair.

"But I couldn't." Lukas said with remorse. With that, Lukas walked away.

Drea watched him leave with a heavy heart. Damion looked at her with a gentle gaze and sighed.

"I've known Lukas for half my life. He's not the best at apologizing. But he owns up to it when he's wrong. He'll come around. Trust me." Said Damion with a slim smile.

Drea nodded as a tear rolled down her cheek. His smile disappeared and he stared at her. "I'm sorry, Drea. For everything." Damion whispered.

Even though it wasn't him she wanted the apology from. It still felt good to hear it. They stood there for a while, silent.

A sound from the woods interrupted their thoughts. They both looked up the ridge. Lukas stood there.

"We should get moving. They lost our trail but we don't have long before they find it again." He said before disappearing back into the trees.

Drea sighed as Damion said, "Let's get moving then."

❄❄❄

Drea walked behind Damion in a stupor, the sun was shining brightly in her eyes. All she could see were the outlines of Damion and Lukas. They had been walking for an entire day. They had passed through a small town but made no effort to stay the night. Drea had been able to purchase some food. Some for herself and Damion. Lukas had declined anything Drea had tried to offer. She had no idea Lukas could be provoked so easily. Damion had seemed to make sure she was never alone with Lukas. For this, she was grateful. Lukas kept his distance from her as well.

❄❄❄

After a few more hours of walking, the sun was beginning to dim. The three of them settled in the woods. They had found a good place to stop.

Drea stared at a spot on the ground that glowed with the little sunlight that was left. Her heart lurched when Lukas came out of the thicket with an armful of branches and twigs. He met her gaze. Lukas looked away when Damion came quickly after him. He looked at Drea then Lukas before placing his own bundle of branches down.

After he was finished building a fire, Damion stood up and walked over to the log Drea sat on. She watched him curiously when she noticed a handkerchief full of something in his hand. Damion let out a chuckle as he handed it to Drea. She gasped. *Berries!*

"Save some for me, please." Joked Damion while he sat down on the dirt and used the log as a backrest.

Drea couldn't make any promises. She was famished. After a few handfuls, the berries were almost gone. Drea tried to chew the berries slowly to help stifle her hunger. She nudged Damion on the shoulder and handed him the rest of the berries.

He gazed at them with hunger, which turned to guilt when Drea's stomach let out a hungry gurgle.

"That's okay. You can have the rest." Said Damion as he closed her fingers gently over the berries.

"Please?" Drea whispered, opening her hand once again.

Damion was about to decline again before Lukas placed another branch into the fire. He let out a sigh and took the berries from her and tossed them into his mouth. Drea rubbed her hand as it began to ache once again.

"Just don't think about it." Said Damion after he noticed her actions. Drea glared at him.

"Like it's that easy." She said as she gazed through the fire and at Lukas. There was a dark purple bruise on his cheek from Damion's punch. Lukas had also dealt a few blows to Damion. His brow had been slit, along with a few bruises around his eye. He noticed her gaze. He smiled and looked away.

"Don't worry. I've had worse." He said before tossing another berry into his mouth. Curious, Drea asked,

"Like what?"

Damion opened his mouth to speak but closed it when Lukas stood and started to walk away.

"Where are you going?" Asked Damion, his voice had an edge. Lukas looked back at him.

"I'll be right back." Said Lukas as he walked off. Damion glanced up at her.

"Does your hand feel better?"

Drea looked at him, surprised. It did. She nodded and glanced down at it. A small black dot was directly in the center of her palm.

"Hmm." She said, "I don't think that was there before."

Damion looked at it with an attentive gaze. He shook his head.

"Could just be a freckle." Damion answered before folding up the handkerchief that had once held the berries.

Drea looked at him, her heart full of doubt.

Drea glanced at her palm to inspect the dot once more.

"I don't think it's a freckle." She stated. Damion nodded as he looked at it again.

"They don't just appear like that," Drea said.

"Maybe you injured yourself and just didn't know it. Could have happened when we were cutting down the trees? Well, if it makes you feel any better, I once got a fish hook caught in my finger, the pain was unbelievable." He said, a sound of distraction in his words as the memory seemed to flash in his head. Drea let out a burst of laughter. Damion glanced up at her as she continued to laugh.

"What?" He asked with a happy tone in his voice.

"A lure?" Drea asked breathlessly. "Now, how did that happen?"

Damion furrowed his brow. "Are you sure you are ready for such a story?"

Drea stared at him, confused. Was it actually a shocking story? Damion laughed when she crossed her legs and looked at him intently.

"Well. It was a long time ago. I was maybe eight years old. My brother, his friends and I had decided to go fishing and bring some fish home in time for dinner. And I hated fishing at the time. I was scared of the water."

"My brother… He reeled in this big trout and had me take out the lure. I did and then the lure slipped and dug into my thumb." Said Damion as he scratched the back of his neck.

"Did it hurt?" Asked Drea, her stomach churned at the thought of having a fish hook caught in her skin. Damion nodded with a distracted smile.

"So why did you do it?" She asked.

"Well, he was my older brother. And younger siblings always, *always* want to be like their older siblings. I did it because I wanted to be like him." Damion said, his voice beginning to shake with grief. Drea stared at him. Before she could ask, he swiped at his eyes.

"He died two weeks after that day. He and his friends had stumbled into a dragon's nesting area. Kilian, he saw the whole thing and ran." Said Damion angrily, as he tugged at a tuft of grass.

"I'm sorry. I shouldn't have asked." Drea said, guilt crept into her heart like a prowling wolf ready to pounce on its prey.

Damion's face went skyward. Drea followed his gaze, the sun had descended deep into the trees, allowing the night sky to take over.

"We should get some rest." He said as he laid down by the log. Drea nodded and flattened out on the top of the log. She heard him take a deep long unsettled breath. Drea sighed and shut her eyes, welcoming the needed sleep.

❄❄❄

Drea woke to Damion shaking her awake. She pushed away his hands.

"What?" She asked while she sat up. Her body ached from sleeping on the log.

"Lukas hasn't come back." Said Damion, fear creeping into his words. Drea stood up and looked around. There was no trace of Lukas. He had left at night and never came back. The sun was already beginning to rise.

"Come on. We have to find him." Said Drea after she grabbed her pack and kicked around the branches of the fire before they set off.

Chapter VIII

Past Echoes

Khan had made it to the White Bridge Kingdom and talked to Lady Helene about the King of Dragons; she was quite delighted to hear about the King of Dragons.

Helene had insisted that Khan should have Cordelia come too. So Lady Helene sent her dragon, Dothrane, to find her. Once the two dragons were back and safe, the people were certainly in a frenzy about a newcomer. Lady Helene had forgotten to warn the people that a new dragon would arrive. Cordelia did not appreciate the attention. It had taken a while for Cordelia to trust Khan again after that. She had thought the uprising against her was his doing. After they began to settle in, Lady Helene had promised to keep the egg safe while Khan went to look for his sister and friends. He had acquired some intel that King Dolion's soldiers were tracking a trio of people heading West. Khan figured he would start there.

❄❄❄

Cordelia's boiling water flame flew out of her mouth as she and Khan circled the line of soldiers.

Cordelia waited to land until she could no longer hear the cries of the soldiers. Khan slid off and bolted toward a soldier who was untouched by Cordelia's boiling brew. The soldier roared, picked up his sword from the ground and launched himself toward Khan. Before

Khan and the soldier reached each other, Cordelia flew past them, swept the soldier up with her left talon and carried him away.

"Cheater!" Khan yelled after his dragon, he shook his head and glanced toward the circle of fallen soldiers.

There was a scorch mark burned into the grass, the fire was still flickering and passing to each blade of grass. Cordelia came and landed beside him.

What is it? Cordelia's question flowed through his head.

"I don't know. I've never seen anything like it." Replied Khan as he squatted to touch the burn mark. He winced and ripped his hand away as it burned him. When he touched it the fire began to rise higher. He backed away.

"That might not have been the best idea." Said Cordelia while she took several steps away from the mark as the flames grew higher.

"Khan, I don't like this." Whispered Cordelia as eerie whispers filled the wind.

"The Mountains will quake and the earth shall melt.

Rivers of Blood and Fire will stain the land.

Bring forth the King.

Bring forth the Dragon."

Khan fell to the ground as an invisible force pulled him to the dirt. His face was inches from the flames. His head pounded as Cordelia cried his name. The fire kept pulling him closer. Khan stared directly into the fire. Images flowed through it.

A battle, no, a war. Innocents were dying. Fire rained down from the sky.

"We should leave." Suggested Cordelia while she looked fearfully to her left and right.

Khan's heart leaped when a familiar face came across the flames.

Drea.

"The Daughter and Son of Fire and Water.

The Daughter must die for the world to live.

The Son must kill to save her life."

After this was said, Khan's vision went black and he was thrown into an empty void of unconsciousness.

❄❄❄

Khan sat up and ashes fell off him like sand. Everything was either in flames or covered in ash and soot.

"Cordelia?" Called Khan while he crawled over to her. She looked like a big lump of barely noticeable blue.

The lump let out a low rumble and shook as Cordelia's head swung around to look at him. Her face was covered in ash. Her eyelashes were now gray. She huffed out of breath of smoke, blowing away the ashes covering Khan's own face.

"I told you. We should have left." Growled Cordelia while she stood and shook the ashes off her body and back onto Khan.

In response, he coughed, waving the dust away. Khan stood shakily. Cordelia gave him her wing tip for support.

"Well, we can—" Khan was swiftly cut off as several cries of fear and anguish echoed in the smoky wind.

Cordelia's ears flicked up and turned toward the sound. "It's this way." She said, waiting for Khan to climb onto her saddle before taking off into the trees.

❄❄❄

Khan and Cordelia stalked carefully through the trees. The cries had died out a few minutes ago. Now the only sound was the sound of silence among the trees. His heart pounded as they approached an old camp place. The smoke and the rustling sound of fire started to eat up the brush and trees around it.

Khan jumped as a scream erupted into the air. Cordelia twisted toward it and took off. They came upon a clearing. Six giant men seemed to have accosted a group of travelers. He recognized the girl among the group with long, miskept black hair while she kicked away her attacker's hands.

"Drea!" He cried as anger and fear began to rise up from his belly. The other two must be Damion and Lukas.

As a response Cordelia took flight and went straight after Drea. The girl screamed when the man was ripped away from her.

Everything fell silent when Cordelia opened her mouth wide and let out a roar that caused Khan to put his hands over his ears. In response, something from the cliff above them came down. Forcing Cordelia to land roughly. Khan slid off her back and to the ground. He quickly drew his sword and leaped into the fray. Damion battled viciously with Lukas by his side.

Khan's heart leaped when quick hands shoved him to the ground. Someone had moved him out of the way of an arrow. A scream filled the air. Khan turned quickly and saw Drea grabbing at her left shoulder. A long, thin arrow was settled on the back of her shoulder blade. Fear eclipsed Khan's heart.

Cordelia, get her out of here! Ordered Khan while he stood and kicked away a charging man.

I have my own problems at the moment. Cordelia's voice drifted into Khan's head.

He turned. Cordelia was backed up against the cliff, three large dogs cornered her. When she opened her mouth to hurl the boiling water at them, they'd turn and run out of range and return when she was out. While Khan was distracted, a man came up behind him.

"Khan, duck!" An early warning tipped Khan off and he was able to easily evade the man. As he dodged, a club came flying and hit the man head on, causing him to fall to the ground unconscious.

Khan turned, Drea stood there with her right arm forward. She had thrown the club. Before he could warn her, a big man came up behind her with a shield and shoved it toward the arrow. Drea cried out in pain and fell to the ground. Immediately thunder and rain clouds rolled into the sky as Khan's heart flooded with vengeance. Silence fell as Cordelia responded to Khan's anger. The sky darkened while her deep growl rumbled in her chest.

The men started to back away and the three dogs took off with their tails between their legs. Rain poured down as Cordelia approached the group of men. They all stood still, like they were hoping she couldn't see them. Thunder and lightning backed Cordelia's roar as she opened her jaws wide. Everything fell silent following her deafening roar. A few seconds later the men turned tail and ran.

"Khan! We can't stop the bleeding!" Cried Damion. He and Lukas were desperately trying to stop the bleeding from Drea's shoulder. The arrow had gone all the way through the top of her shoulder.

"Is there enough time to make it to White Bridge?" Asked Khan as he ran over to them. Cordelia came quickly behind him.

Lukas glanced at him before he side-eyed Damion whose attention was intensely on Drea.

"Only if it's just you and her. The dragon at full speed should get you there. But I can't say for sure if she will make it." Said Lukas while he gently held Drea's head and Damion lifted her off the ground with a grunt.

Khan quickly jumped onto Cordelia's saddle when she bowed to let him on. Damion handed Drea carefully over to Khan who took her with great concern. Damion placed a hand on Cordelia's shoulder as she stood.

"Go quickly." Said Lukas just before Cordelia took flight.

❄❄❄

"Come on Cordelia! Go!" Yelled Khan urging Cordelia on while he stared down at Drea.

Her color was getting paler. She was losing too much blood. Cordelia's speed increased as she thrust her feet and talons through the air, her wings flapping as fast as they could. Khan's heart skipped a beat when the beautiful white castle came into view. Drea groaned and her eyes fluttered.

"No, no, no. Stay with me, Drea. Stay with me." Whispered Khan when her eyes closed shut. Her face contorted with pain.

"Go, go, go!" He shouted when her breathing became short and shallow.

❄❄❄

Khan waited outside the infirmary, his heart was in his throat as he awaited for news. It had been several hours since Khan had brought Drea to White Bridge. Cordelia waited beside him. Her anxiety was feeding on his anxiety. Her head rested on her talons like a dog would lay their head on their paws. Silas came up and sat beside him. Khan straightened and cleared his throat. The man had just come back from night service at White Bridge's ancestral church.

"She's going to be alright, Khan. Just breathe." Said Silas with kindness in his voice.

"Helene has made absolutely sure Drea had the best care from our doctors." Comforted Silas when Khan rubbed his eyes with exhaustion.

Cordelia's big head came up onto Khan's lap. She gazed up at him.

"I'm sure she'll be okay. If she's anything like you. She will be." Cordelia assured before pulling away. Silas watched her, even though he didn't understand Cordelia's language, he knew exactly what she had intended to say. Silas patted Khan on the shoulder twice before he got up and walked toward the castle. Khan sighed. *Drea is nothing like me.* He told himself in his head and flinched when Cordelia looked up at him. He cleared his throat when Lady Helene's daughter, Lily, walked by. Her satin dress trailing on the stone behind her.

"Khan." Said Lily, bowing her head as she walked by.

"Lily." Greeted Khan when she passed by. Her brother, Thomas walked behind her. He stopped before he reached Khan and let her go ahead. Khan was older than Lily, but Thomas had a good two years on Khan. Even so, his face was riddled with worry.

"I know you're worried, Khan, but you can't spend the whole night up and waiting for news." Said Thomas, his hands in his pockets.

Khan rubbed his hands together when Thomas clapped his hand on Khan's shoulder before walking away to find his sister. He watched him leave. *Silas and Thomas, like father, like son,* thought Khan. Both had a protective and sensitive nature.

"Khan, they're right. It won't do anyone any good if you drop from exhaustion." Said Cordelia as she stood and nudged him up.

Khan nodded and walked beside her as they made their way to the castle. Something rustled behind them. Khan turned quickly out of fear. Lady Helene's dragon, Dothrane, walked toward them. This dragon was a whole foot bigger than Cordelia. Every time the mighty beast stepped, there was a disturbance in the ground. Like the stone and earth were ready to bend to Dothrane's will. Without glancing at Khan, he passed in between Khan and Cordelia. Dothrane's long tail wrapped around Cordelia's neck to pull her toward his stable. While Khan slept in the castle, Cordelia shared a little pond with Dothrane in the stable area. He waved her goodbye before jogging toward the castle doors.

❄❄❄

The next morning Khan awoke to the sound of birds singing and the cold chill against his skin. He sat up in his bed and gazed around his room. A knock came at his door.

"Come in." He muttered while he shifted out of his bed. Khan pulled on his socks and got out of bed just as Silas and Thomas walked in.

"Any news?" Asked Khan, pulling a long wool shirt over his head. Both Thomas and Silas shook their heads, leaving Khan downcast and upset. Before he could say anything, Thomas said,

"We're going to go fishing. You should come."

Khan was about to turn the offer down but Silas placed his hand on Khan's shoulder and stared at him sincerely.

"We figured you could use some time in nature. Cordelia can go with or stay and rest with Dothrane." He said, Khan looked at him and nodded vaguely.

Silas and Thomas smiled and clapped Khan on the shoulder before walking out of his room to leave him to get ready. Khan groaned and fell back into his bed. He felt so helpless.

❄❄❄

"Where are you three going?" Asked Lily as she came down the steps of the castle with ease and grace.

"Fishing." Said Silas. Thomas ran up to his sister and poked her.

"Do you want to come?" He asked with a hint of mischief in his voice. Lily stepped away from him with annoyance in her glare, though there was a smile on his face when she slapped away his hands.

"Oh, now, now. You know I don't enjoy such things." Said Lily while she straightened her dress. Khan looked away to roll his eyes.

When he turned back, she was beside him.

"Are you leaving Cordelia?" She asked, a great amount of merriment in her voice. Khan pondered her question. He had driven Cordelia hard the last few days. It would do her some good to get some rest.

"Sure." He said after a long thoughtful pause. Lily clapped her hands together and giggled gleefully before skipping away to the door that led outside to Dothrane's stable.

Khan watched her leave.

"I take it she likes dragons?" He asked when he looked back to Silas and Thomas. They both nodded and smiled.

"She dotes on them whenever she can." Confirmed Silas as he grabbed the fishing poles and Thomas grabbed the box that held fishing lures and bait. Khan sighed and grabbed the bag of food before walking after them.

❄❄❄

Khan sat on the cold, dewy stone while Silas and Thomas conversed.

"But since dragons can speak. Does that mean that other creatures can too?" Asked Thomas before taking a bite of his ham and cheese sandwich.

"Mm-m. No. Dragons are mythical beings. Man was given a gift. Dragons of the Ancients, before our time, decided to help man along." Stated Silas, baiting another lure. Curious, Khan looked back at him.

"The Dragons of the Ancients? What does that mean?" Asked Khan.

"The First Dragons." Said Silas, when he saw that Khan showed no inkling that he knew what Silas was talking about.

"Were you never told that story?" Asked Silas before settling down on the grass.

"Well, time for a lesson of our history." Grunted Thomas as he plopped down beside his father.

"At the beginning of our time, mankind was created. After a while, that time period's method of ruling subjects was basically killing anyone who stood in their way to becoming King. The Ancients did not agree with or like this method. Whenever they tried to commune with mankind, mankind wouldn't listen.

"So, things just got worse from then on." Said Silas, he paused to take a sip of his brandy.

"What happened then?" Asked Khan impatiently. Silas laughed and continued with his story.

"When the Ancients were about to wipe out mankind, one of the Ancient's stepped forward and declared that she would sacrifice herself in order to save mankind. Through all the bad and horrible things man had done, this Ancient had fallen in love with their lust for life and power." Said Silas then took a bite of his sandwich.

Khan pondered on this part of the story. "What was the Ancient's name?" He asked. Before Silas could answer, Thomas beat him to it.

"Nakita." Before he could continue, Silas cut in.

"But instead of sacrificing herself, the Ancients decided to grant her a life in the world of man along with a few other Ancients volunteers. From then on, those four Ancients were to be reborn in the world of men as dragons. When they were reborn, they had no recollection of what or who they were. Each dragon represented an element. Air, fire, water and earth. But we don't know which ones represent which." Stated Silas.

"Now, Nakita, when she was old enough, the Ancients decided to gift her to a man. His name was Ankur. He was the heir to the Kingdom of Orinshire, noble and true. Special to some, harmful to most. But the Ancients chose him to rule over the *entire* Kingdom of Sonerian. They had communed with a woman and told her of the prophecy. Whoever Nakita was gifted to would rule over the world. And surprisingly everyone obeyed the Ancients. Of course, after a while, new places were discovered across the seas and great oceans and many abandoned Nakita's and Ankur's rule. Nakita and her *kyros's* descendants have ruled over the country of Sonerian for more than one hundred years." Finished Silas.

"It is said that her descendants had ruled over the country of Sonerian all the way up to this lifetime. Which was hundreds of years ago." Said Thomas before casting out his fishing line.

"Really?" Asked Khan, disbelief filling his words. Both nodded with a grim frown. They seemed to know all too well of who their ruler was.

"So does that mean King Dolion had a dragon? And it was a descendant of Nakita?" Asked Khan, fully intrigued by this story.

"How are we sure that the dragon is a descendant?" Asked Khan, none of this logic made sense.

"Green eyes that look like fire and a similarity with names." Said Silas. Thomas reeled in his fishing line.

"But the dragon's lineage is also said to be broken. That it's meant to be broken." Thomas stated before baiting the lure again.

While Khan pondered on this, his thoughts drifted to Thomas's statement. *Was this line of dragons that ruled meant to be broken? And if it was, by whom?*

Chapter IX

Gone Again

A few days after Khan had brought Drea to receive medical help in White Bridge, Khan had finally acquired news of her condition. She had finally responded to treatment and her shoulder wound would soon be healed after some undisturbed rest. Silas and Thomas had done all they could to keep Khan's worried and anxious mind off of Drea. For the most part, they succeeded, but Drea was still always in the back of his mind.

"Khan?" Asked a concerned Lily from across the table. Thomas glanced up from his lunch. Khan jumped and looked at her. Her eyebrow was raised.

"You haven't touched your plate." She said while looking at Khan's full plate of food. He glanced at it before chewing on his fingernails and staring out the window.

"I'm not hungry." He said. Thomas dropped his utensils and ran his fingers through his long, brown hair.

"That's the second plate you've turned down today." Stated Thomas before crossing his arms and glaring at Khan. Khan stared back defensively. A hand being slammed on the table broke the awkward and somewhat hostile silence.

The three looked to see Silas at the end of the table. His face contorted with anger and fear when a messenger whispered something into his ear. Helene stared at him from the other end of the table. Silas looked up at her, his fingers tapped the table nervously. Helene stood up.

"Children. Please leave us." Said Helene while she walked over to her husband. Khan looked at Lily and Thomas before getting out of his seat and heading out the door with them. As Thomas sped down the corridor, he left Lily and Khan far behind. Lily stopped Khan in his tracks. Her gaze was scared and anxious.

"You should go check on Drea. I have a feeling that things may not go well tonight." She whispered, her gray eyes wide as she stared up at him. He was clearly puzzled by what she said, but Khan decided to listen to her advice.

❄❄❄

Khan opened the door that led into the infirmary and walked in cautiously. Nurses and medics looked at him and nodded before going back to seeing their patients. He made his way to where the injured were held in the back room of the building. His heart quickened as he looked around the room and found Drea's cot empty. He began desperately searching for Drea or any sign of her.

"Are you looking for someone?" Asked a voice from behind Khan, he quickly turned around and saw a short woman looking up at him, sheets and cloths in her arms. It took Khan a moment to regain his composure.

"Uh. Yes, Drea." Khan said, his voice shaky. The woman nodded and said,

"I believe she had made her way down to the stables."

❄❄❄

Khan quickly made his way down to the stables in a panic. He had accidentally plowed over two guards who had just wanted to have their break in peace. He stopped a few feet away from the stables out of breath. He let out a quick scream when Cordelia landed beside him.

"What? You didn't hear me coming?" She asked when she saw how rattled Khan was at her arrival. Khan shuddered, in his blind rush of fear, he had been cut off from Cordelia.

"Oh." She muttered when his thoughts drifted into her head.

Khan stared at her for a second before walking forward to the stables with Cordelia by his side. Khan and Cordelia entered Dothrane's stable. The large dragon was lying on the hay like a massive dog would lay, his head bowed low. A girl was there in front of Dothrane, her hand outstretched to touch his snout. The dragon bowed his head lower to allow Drea to almost hold his giant head in her arms.

Whoa. I've never seen him do that before. Not even with Helene or Lily. Echoed Cordelia's voice in Khan's head while he stared flabbergasted at Drea and Dothrane. The dragon let out a gentle moan and shut his eyes while Drea ran the palm of her hand up and down the long bridge of Dothrane's snout. The dragon let out a rhythmic hum that sounded like birdsong. Khan watched with admiration as a branch from the small tree by the pond stretched out to Drea.

The dragon pulled away when the branch twirled around Drea. She let out a laugh when the branch stretched in front of her. There was a beautiful red rose that grew right in front of her. Dothrane let out a breath of mist onto the flower. The beautiful flower rose tall as it was dusted with a white sheet of small crystallized leaves. The dragon seemed to smile when Drea picked the rose gently from the branch. Khan gulped when the dragon looked at him and Cordelia once he finally saw them. Dothrane let out a rumbling growl and stood up. Hay fell off the leaves and twigs that made up the dragon's body. As quick as a river the dragon lifted itself up and flew up into the air before gliding toward the castle.

Khan looked back at Drea who stared after the dragon.

"I've never seen him like that with anyone. Neither has Cordelia." Said Khan, causing Drea to look at him. They circled each other slowly, both filled with curiosity.

"What happened to your face?" Asked Drea, Khan shrugged.

"Cordelia. But it was an accident." Stated Khan while he scratched the back of his neck. Drea stopped in awe in front of Cordelia. "Cordelia." Drea said simply.

The dragon nodded with caution. Drea smiled and walked up to her, the rose still in between her fingers.

❄❄❄

Khan stood leaning against the stable door and watched his sister silently as she circled Cordelia. The dragon was full of disdain. Even though Drea was Khan's sister, Cordelia hated her with every fiber of her being. Cordelia pulled away and let out a trilling hiss as Drea trailed her hand along her tail.

If she keeps touching me like this, you may not have a sister soon. Khan let out a scoff at the dragon's thought.

Lily is with you practically every day and you seem to be fine with her. Khan jeered into Cordelia's head.

The dragon gaped at him before her voice floated into his mind. *Lily respects space. So, this is different.*

Just take it easy. Admonished Khan.

"She's beautiful, Khan." Said Drea, a great hint of amazement behind her words.

Khan cocked his head and stared at her, happy that she seemed to approve of Cordelia. He shoved Cordelia's whispers out of his mind and shut his mind off from hers. With the help of Lady Helene, he learned how exactly to do that.

It had been nearly a week since Khan brought Drea back, she seemed cautious of the kingdom. Khan pulled away from the door and walked toward Drea, her face full of amazement as she continued to look Cordelia over. He smiled as he saw Cordelia's disgust.

"Would you like to ride her?" proposed Khan.

Cordelia's head jerked toward him, almost in an instant, she was gone and into the clouds. Drea let out a shocked gasp and stared after Cordelia.

"Did she just..."

Khan nodded and put his hands in his pockets. It was probably for the best, Drea didn't like heights. Drea threw her hands up in defeat and headed back to the stables. Khan sighed as she walked past him. He watched her as she opened the door and gazed at the egg laying in a cradle of hay.

"So this is what everything is about?" Shouted Drea as she looked at it.

"Yeah. Apparently, it's the *King of Dragons*?" Shouted Khan back as he fumbled with his cloak string.

Drea acknowledged him with a grunt and shut the door. Khan grew pensive and cursed under his breath, he needed to make things right with his sister, if there was ever anything wrong. She had been elusive concerning anything about Lukas, and Damion. What did she go through when they were separated? He sighed, maybe he should ask?

"Drea... Can we talk about...?" Khan started, he stopped as he heard Drea hiss from inside, "Leave me alone about that!"

Khan groaned and started toward the stable door. She'd have to communicate sooner or later.

"Drea, come on." pushed Khan gently.

"Leave me alone!" She repeated in exasperation.

"Drea..." Khan started, his words slowly seemed to slip away as the sound of marching and the rattle of armor filled the air.

Drea seemed to hear it too; she walked out the door, stopped beside Khan and looked toward the coming procession. They both ducked in response to a large black dragon swooping down just above them. Then they heard a loud booming roar in the air above. Drea came up close behind Khan. He could sense her fear.

The air stilled as Lady Helene slowly came into the small garden and faced them. Fear, guilt, and shame shone in her eyes and on her face. Soldiers wearing red and black flowed in behind her. The large dragon set down heavily in an open space in the garden, and a tall man slid down from the dragons and marched deliberately through the soldiers toward them. Drea was in shock and felt disgust when she saw his face illuminated by the sun, showing off his features. He appeared to be a good five years older than Khan. Khan grimaced at his face; his jawline was sharp, his cheekbones harsh. Three thick, long scars traveled from a horribly mauled cheek to beneath his armor. Khan guessed he didn't look much different from himself, to say the least. When Drea saw Khan again, the first thing she did was stare at the scar along his face.

"Can we help you with something?" Asked Khan defiantly.

The man's eyes drifted to Khan. Khan looked away, unable to hold his gaze. The man's eyes shifted to Drea as he circled them in silence.

"I said, can we help you?" Added Khan annoyingly as the man stopped directly in front of him.

In an instant, the man thrust his fist into Khan's stomach. He grunted in pain, clutched his stomach and bent over, trying to catch his breath. The man looked past him and back at Drea.

"You'd be wise to communicate." Said the man gently.

He turned and ordered one of the soldiers to search the barn. *Why did he keep looking at Drea?* Khan wondered. Instinctively, Khan blocked his view of her. The man's eyes drifted to Khan once more. Khan's heart sank when the soldier came out of the barn with the egg in his hands.

"No." Whispered Khan watching the man take the egg with surprise.

The dragon roared and flapped its wings while the man examined the egg. They knew what it was.

The man glanced back at Drea, shook his head and pointed a finger at her.

"You're supposed to be dead." Said the man while he straightened.

Khan's heart skipped a beat. Why didn't Drea ever tell him who she had encountered?

The soldiers fanned out, surrounding Khan and Drea. "Can't you just leave us alone? You have the egg, we won't cause you any trouble if you let us go." Stated Khan as thunder began to hum lightly. The man tossed up his hand dismissively and walked toward his dragon.

"Take him!" Ordered the man.

Khan was shoved to the ground before he had a chance to react. Drea was pulled from him in an instant. Khan twisted and tried to fight back. The soldiers grabbed him by the arms and pulled him up. Drea was being forced roughly to her knees.

"You have them now. Will you let my children go?" Asked Lady Helene, her voice quivering. "No." The man stated plainly.

"You harbored fugitives of the King, my lady. I'm afraid that makes you guilty of treason."

Khan roared, then lightning struck close by the man's feet, causing him to take a few steps backwards. Drea called her brother's name as she was being pulled roughly away. Without any warning, flames struck several of the guards, causing confusion. The fire had come out of nowhere. Khan looked at Drea one last time, before blackness invaded his vision.

Chapter X

Beginning of the End

Cordelia flew away hurriedly from the horrible scene that lay before her. She thought that she and Khan would be safe here. Clearly, they could not stay any longer. The only reasonable thing to do would be to rescue Khan, but Cordelia didn't even know where to start, or if she even could. She couldn't launch a full-scale rescue by herself, she would need help. Cordelia felt helpless. What would happen to Khan? In that instant, she realized she did have help. Atlas. She knew where he would be.

❄❄❄

After a long flight, she crossed into the Reedling waters and dove straight into the depths. Minutes later, she found Atlas in his sea cave. She explained the situation and pleaded for help.

"I can't do that, Cordelia." Atlas stammered as he swam away from her.

"Why not?" Groaned Cordelia, chasing after him. "We can't invoke violence toward Man, only the under-dwellers." Answered Atlas.

"Surely, you can do something?" she said, following after him.

Atlas stopped and looked back at her, his eyes full of sorrow.

"Cordelia, last time we interfered with Man, our kind was massacred, not just above but below as well."

Cordelia stared at him in astonishment. Was he talking from his own experiences?

Atlas shrugged and hung his head in self-pity. He didn't say anything but Cordelia could guess what his silence meant.

"I'm sorry, I never realized..." Cordelia started but shut her mouth as Atlas waved his talons and swam briskly away.

She followed him and decided it was best to not interfere with his thoughts. Cordelia thought the fact that his egg was so close to hatching couldn't help either.

Cordelia turned and swam toward the Monarch's den. She figured she could at least ask him. The Monarch was a mighty Sea dragon, something Cordelia didn't think could exist. He had giant wings and a bellow that would shake the waves into a frenzy.

Like Atlas, many of the Reedlings could hear outsiders' thoughts. The Monarch was one of them.

"Greetings, Cordelia." The Monarch said in greeting.

Cordelia twisted to see the Monarch behind her. His whiskers trailed far behind him, his eyes lively despite his age. She cocked her head at him, wondering if he could hear her thoughts now. The Monarch's ears twitched, and as his eyes looked at her up and down, he nodded and softly glided past her.

"I'm afraid we cannot help you with that, my dear." Said the Monarch as he glanced back at her. "B-- Why not?" Cordelia asked.

"Man would slaughter us once they figure out where we are." Continued the Monarch.

"Surely, there's something you could do? Anything?" She countered.

The Monarch shook his head in a gentle way and softly touched Cordelia's forehead with his large snout. She sighed; that was the Reedling's way of asking for forgiveness. Cordelia nodded and bowed her head, then slowly turned and fluttered away. It was worth a shot. Cordelia shot, and she missed.

❄❄❄

The horrifying sounds of armor and swords clashing filled the air. Cordelia fought from above, fleeing from loose arrows and the hot breath of fire. Khan and his army fought hard below. They were losing.

Cordelia trilled in fear. Khan and three other men were forced onto their knees. A large man came toward them. The man wore a golden crown on his head. Cordelia's body went cold. An enormous, pitch-black dragon followed slowly behind him. She recognized this type of dragon. It was from the Cave of Memories. It's in the paintings that the Elders drew on the walls and ceilings. It had no front arms, the dragon's wings acted as arms. Cordelia's breath caught in her throat. The *Black Death* has returned.

Cordelia watched from the safety of the clouds. The man pointed a finger, that seemed to be dripping in black ooze, at the four men. He moved out of the way while Khan and the three other men cowered in fear at the sight of the dragon. Cordelia's heart stopped when the dragon opened its mouth. Black ooze slowly fell from its jaws. The dragon's chest expanded and gazed down at the four men. With a roar, black ooze spilled like a waterfall over top of the four men.

"No!" Cordelia cried from the sky. Folding her wings, she dived. She roared as something green-blue streaked past her. The speed of this thing sent her tumbling in the air. By the time she was upright and steady, the black ooze fell on the green-blue creature.

It didn't even cry out in pain, but instead flew effortlessly away.

Before she could figure out what had happened, a black blanket shadowed her vision. She was plunged into darkness when a loud voice invaded her mind.

"The end is near, young one.

Embrace it, or all will fall."

❄❄❄

Cordelia woke with a start, shaking her head to clear it. It must have been a dream, she thought. She took a deep breath, and it caught in her throat as she saw Atlas staring at her anxiously.

"What? Has something happened?" Asked Cordelia as she blinked away the blurriness. "Yes and no," he said.

Cordelia let out a gentle grunt as she stretched her still tired limbs and followed Atlas to the bed of reeds where his egg rested.

"It moved." Said Atlas, staring at the egg as if it were made of glass.

"It moved? Atlas, that's not really something to..." Started Cordelia, "To worry about? Yeah, believe me, I know it's not." Finished Atlas.

Cordelia gazed at him cautiously, she didn't know how to handle this problem. Was he so really afraid of his egg hatching?

"Ha, I guess I am. Funny, huh?" Atlas spoke, answering her thoughts out loud.

Cordelia cursed under her breath, he wasn't meant to hear that. She should have been more delicate with her thoughts.

"Yes, you should have!" Snapped Atlas.

Cordelia trilled and pulled away from him in fear and surprise. She knew it wasn't the best idea to mess with a drake when their egg was close to hatching and while the mother was gone, or dead. Immediately, Atlas looked away from her, with sadness and pain shining in the depths of his eyes. He gently touched his snout to her forehead before gliding away. Cordelia sighed, he hadn't been forthcoming with her since she mentioned the King of Dragons. Maybe, the reason why every dragon fears it, is because it's what they were taught. Maybe, some dragons would like to stay in power and thought when the King of Dragons came, they'd be nothing.

There were paintings in the Forgotten Cove in Waterling territory that tell the prophecy of three. A boy, a mythical beast called a Chowla'ri, and the King of Dragons. In those stories, it says that once the King of Dragons is born, he will rise and become the highest of all dragons. Every Flight would become one. No need for a monarchy or tyranny in some Flights.

She shook her head. Struggling to clear her thoughts, she swam to the surface. Cordelia stared at her reflection once more. She had grown a lot more than she had thought. Her muscles were almost double in size. Then again, being on the run and fighting tends to change things. She could see that her horns had become thicker and longer, her eyes could show stories some may not believe. After all, eyes are the opening to one's soul and there were things that she wished wouldn't have happened or that she could somehow forget.

But nevertheless, they were there; her scars, inside and out. She continued gazing at her reflection on the still surface of the water. She could see several battle wounds along her sleek form. Each one with its own story. The largest one was on her left side just above her shoulder, where the scales were missing, revealing the dull, tan hide beneath. Cordelia turned away from her reflection, it saddened her to know that she was no longer the dragon she once knew.

Images of Khan flickered through her mind as she slithered back to Atlas's den. It felt like it had been so long since he was taken by the soldiers, but it was only two days ago. Cordelia sighed heavily and laid down in her bed of reeds before closing her eyes and wishing for a peaceful round of rest.

Chapter XI

Shimmering Stallions

Drea stared numbly at the dusty walls of the room that now held her captive. Her head pounded as thoughts overwhelmed her. So many dreams, so many nightmares troubled her mind. The only thing that remained constant in these dreams was the desert and the red dragon, along with unbelievable bloodshed.

She and Khan had both been captured and worse than that, separated.

Malakai, the Great King's son, had taken her to the King's lesser palace. They believed that she was responsible for the fire that set some soldiers ablaze when they captured Khan. Maybe she was, maybe she wasn't. If she were asked, she wouldn't know how to answer the question.

Drea sat up in her bed and drew her knees to her chest. She felt sick with hopelessness. Everything felt so bleak, and it seemed like her bad luck would never end.

Her body ached from the beatings she had received from the guards after she tried to strangle a few of them when they got too close to her. Drea was a lot weaker than she had once been, or the people she hurt were weaker than these guards, a lot weaker. Sadly enough, she couldn't learn which battles she should run from or fight. Every time she had chosen to fight, which seemed like the right idea, she'd end up hurt or captured.

Drea was pulled from her melancholy thoughts as Malakai and two soldiers stopped at her cell door, but not too close. Malakai shook his head, meaning for her to see. He heard what she had done to the guards who had gotten too close to her cell door.

"Learned our lesson then, have we?" Asked Malakai, anger cut through his words like a knife.

"Which one was that?" Asked Drea as she laid her head on the wall so she could face the ceilings. She covered her concern with a sigh when she heard the door open with a clank. Her ears burned anxiously, waiting for the rattling sound of armor and the click of boots. Instead, she heard the gentle padding of bare feet touching the brick floor.

Drea shut her eyes, waiting to see what Malakai had planned for her this time. She couldn't help but flinch as two cold hands gently touched hers. The hands traveled to her neck and then to her cheeks. She let the hands tilt her head downward to face away from the ceiling to face them.

"Dr-- Drea?"

Drea slowly peeked, then her eyes flashed open as she recognized Damion's gentle eyes beneath a thick mass of dirty hair. As swift as she could, Drea threw her arms around him and squeezed with all her might. She still didn't like the man but seeing him safe made her feel some joy. Strong hands reached down and roughly tore the two apart. Drea cried out as the fingers jabbed into old wounds, threatening to reopen them.

"Easy with her. She's too fragile right now." Said the gentle voice of the prince.

Drea glared openly at him. She hoped the hatred and anger hid the pain and sorrow behind her gaze. He pondered the outcome, then glanced at Damion, who was held back by the two soldiers. The prince had a look of frustration and deep concentration on his face.

"We can try to crack her a little bit more." One guard said harshly.

Drea barely had time to react before the guard kicked her in the stomach. She cried out in pain and was flung backward from the power of the blow.

Before she could catch her breath, the prince took hold of her hair and pulled her up. She tugged at his hands, trying to pull them away. She could feel her hair beginning to tear from its roots. She groaned and dropped roughly to the ground, taking a knee to her face. She could already feel the blood traveling down her face and neck. Her heart ached for Damion, who was being pulled roughly out of her cell. Muffled cries were heard as he was pulled out of her cell. The prince came around to her once more.

She forced out her hands and slowly crawled away. "Please." She begged, "No more. Please, no more."

Her pleas fell on deaf ears as the remaining guard grabbed her hair once more and pulled her to her feet. She groaned as he lifted a fist, ready to strike.

Darkness began to close in on her, but swiftly receded the moment a cool blade tip touched her belly. Her arms were now against the guard's chest. She tried to push him away, but in the end, it would all be in vain. For a moment, everything fell silent and still as her eyes locked with his.

Drea couldn't fight back even if she wanted to. Usually, the guards wouldn't take it this far.

She was brought back to reality when she felt the tip of the blade begin to break past her skin. With all her might, she kept the guard's knife at bay, holding his gaze.

Her look of defiance only enraged him, but she couldn't seem to let herself look away. Something full of pain flickered behind his brown eyes as he continued to force the knife forward. Suddenly, the guard went limp and fell into Drea. The knife went clattering to the floor.

Drea stared at him as he stared at her, their faces just inches apart. She gasped and shoved the guard away as his skin began to turn gray. Drea jumped when the guard hit the brick floor with a thud.

"Hmm." Muttered the prince. He stood a few feet away with his eyes concentrated hard on the guard.

His face relaxed. The guard's skin color went back to its normal color. He woke up coughing and hacking. Drea clung to the wall as the guard struggled to stand.

"Pathetic." Said Malakai as he helped the guard up before walking out.

The guard walked fearfully after him.

Exhaustion claimed her, she dropped to the floor and closed her eyes in pain. The door slammed shut and the sound of receding footsteps echoed in the small hall. The prince had wanted her dead before, why not let the guard finish his job?

Relieved she was still alive, Drea leaned her head against the wall and shut her eyes. The light was beginning to fade and a familiar headache began to take over her consciousness.

Drea woke slowly to the sound of a gentle, hot breeze. She was leaning against an old white tree, sand and rocks expanded out from its massive trunk. She sat up in surprise and gazed around, taking in her surroundings.

To the West, a slim but tall mountain blossomed out of the ground and into the clouds. As soon as the heat touched her, sweat began to form on her forehead. She did not recognize this landscape. She started to get up from her spot under the tree when a distant roar boomed through the desolate land.

Drea stood up drearily and stumbled forward. As if it were a response, a large shadow covered her from the sun. She looked up and was driven backward by a rough gust of wind. Trying to establish her footing once more she stopped in her tracks.

A lean but muscular dragon landed right in front of her.

"I remember you." Whispered Drea as the dragon looked her over.

It had dark blue eyes and its gaze seemed to penetrate her very soul. It somehow seemed different from when she last saw it. Slowly, the dragon began to bow its head, allowing the sun to shine harshly down on her once again.

Blinded, Drea covered her eyes and turned away. Ever so slowly, darkness began to eclipse Drea's sight. Once she uncovered her eyes, she was in a lowly lit cave of some sort. She couldn't tell for sure, but the roof of the cave seemed to rise indefinitely. It was the largest cave she's ever been in. Along the walls were red and green vines. Just then a loud, forceful burst of warm air erupted above her, causing her hair to ruffle.

Drea looked up to see what had caused the sudden wind and was surprised to see a much larger dragon than the one she just encountered. She stepped back when its large head swooped down and gazed at her.

Its eyes were a steady white and gray, and half of one horn was missing. Its scales were aged roughly from the dust and heat. It was hard to make out in the dim light, but its color looked to be a dull red and purple mixture. Though it seemed to be blind, the dragon gazed directly into her eyes. Gentle, rhythmic beats sounded quietly around her and the cave walls and ceiling began to fall away. It was night. Drea glanced around, several white glowing orbs descended from the shining sky. Heat beamed onto Drea's skin as the orbs touched the earth and lit up the world with luminescent light. She felt something she hadn't felt since, well, since before she could remember. But the feeling she felt now was one that she had felt before somewhere deep in her memory.

"*See.*" Hissed the dragon. Drea's head pounded with a familiar pain while black once again rimmed her vision.

Images of her mother and father filtered through her gaze as the light began to diminish. She could make out the spark of gold in her mother's red hair, and the bright glint of her father's eyes. They must have been young this time. Her mother's face reminded her of a bright sunny morning and her cheeks blushed with gentle tinges of rose when Drea's father walked over to her.

Was this a memory of hers? Drea shook her head, she didn't believe it to be her own. Drea shoved the thought away from her mind as the image faded into another. This time, her parents were riding two beautiful chestnut stallions. Their coats were so clean and well groomed that they shimmered just like the sun.

Suddenly, the images faded, never allowing Drea a good glance at their faces. A new image emerged and became a cluster of burning flames. At dead center was a beautiful manor being consumed by these relentless flames that licked up every inch of vegetation. Then, a dark form burst from the flames and flew up into the sky.

Just then, Drea slipped on a slippery stone, disrupting the image. The dragon's giant head swooped down inches from her face, causing her to plop roughly down in a pool of water. The dragon gazed at her with its dull eyes and cocked its head. Her breath caught in her throat. The dull white and gray in the dragon's eyes slowly faded away. Drea's heart leaped as the eyes reflected the stars with mixtures of blue and pink.

"To see the truth. Find where one remains."

Hissed the dragon. Then everything went black.

PART V
BEGINNING OF FIRE AND WATER

Chapter I

A Burst of Water

Khan stared bluntly at the bright, golden egg. Shame overwhelming him as the Great King Dolion circled it. King Dolion stood facing Khan with his hands behind his back. He was much more terrifying in person than one would expect.

"Tell me, how did you come by this egg?" Chortled the King as he paced around the egg once more.

"It's the same as last time. I found it washed up on a shore." Stated Khan.

"Only a *wyvern kyros* could find this Egg." Growled the King.

Khan did not understand the King's words. The King saw the confusion in Khan's expression and said,

"Where is your dragon?"

"I don't have one." Said Khan simply.

The King roared, catching Khan off guard, drew his sword and swung it across Khan's cheek. Khan slapped his palm over it as it began to bleed. The cut was right over the scar he had suffered from Cordelia.

"You have the scar!" Shrieked the King as he ran his fingers over his own three scars and blind eye. Khan shivered, whatever dragon did that, Khan didn't want to meet. He was suddenly grateful Cordelia had been so gentle.

Khan's anger was kindled inside him when he saw the King's son, Malakai, charge in, his black, dirty boots clicking against the marble flooring. Khan desperately watched to see if anyone would follow behind him, allowing himself false hope.

When the door shut loudly behind the prince, Khan hung his head in disappointment. Where had they taken Drea? Was she okay?

Khan waited anxiously as the King listened to what his son whispered in his ear as he sat on his throne.

The King bellowed at his son, who quickly twirled away from him, causing Khan to jump in surprise.

"You *what*?!" Moaned the King as he gaped at his son in astonishment.

With his head held high, the prince clenched his jaw harshly and somehow kept his composure as the King continued to throw insults at him.

Seeing as the prince wasn't going to answer the insults, the King made a hissing sound and glanced at the egg.

Still chained to the floor, Khan's eyes flicked to the prince's as he felt his gaze on him. His eyes were cold and full of hatred. Khan broke his gaze off from the prince when the King directed another question to him.

"Do you know who you are, boy?" Said the King bitterly.

Khan looked at him in surprise. Malakai glowered at him with fear and hate. Khan shook his head, unsure of where the King was going with this, but he said nothing.

Just as the King opened his mouth to speak, two well-built guardsmen burst into the throne room.

"Yes?" King Dolion impatiently asked.

"We have a situation. A group of peasants are rioting in the city streets, writing symbols along the walls of the streets throughout the kingdom." One of the guards stated matter-of-factly.

The King stared hard at the guard, and asked, "What symbol do they paint?"

The guardsmen glanced at each other uneasily. The two guards separated, turned toward the doors and opened them wide. They held the doors open to allow five more guardsmen to carry in a giant slab of stone with an intricate but distinct marking upon it. Malakai let out a horrified gasp.

A look of disbelief on his face, Khan couldn't help but notice the sear mark on Malakai's neck.

His thoughts were quickly brought back to the issue at hand.

"The myth. The Golden Dragon of the Ancients. They are chanting his coming, sire." Voiced out one of the guardsmen, an edge of fear lining his words.

The King traced the swirling gold-white dragon image on the stone with his fingers. The dragon had white, gold and red fire circling it. What did the guard mean?

Who were the 'Ancients?' Khan slapped his hands over his nose as the foul smell filled the air that Khan had never smelled in his life. The King backed away instantly from the slab. The tips of his fingers were dripping with black ooze. King Dolion had a harsh look of pure hatred on his face as he stomped back to his throne. Glaring at the egg, he sat down on the red cushion.

Just then, something caused the guards to drop the slab and hit the marble floor with a loud crack and it shattered into thousands of pieces.

“Take him. See what else you can get out of him, my son.” Ordered the King. Khan couldn't help but feel his blood boil every time he heard the King speak.

Khan shook his head, there was something about the King that seemed familiar to him. As he thought about this, the prince's hard, icy fingers latched tight on his lower arm and pulled him up off the chain, allowing one of the guards to unlock his shackles. Being dragged by the King’s son, Khan had to hold his breath as he stumbled past the broken remains of the stone.

❄❄❄

Water splashed across Khan’s face, waking him from his troubled sleep with a start. He groaned and struggled against the outstretched hands that grabbed and tugged at him.

The past few days, or what seemed to be days, Khan couldn't keep track anymore, the prince and his henchmen continued to batter and whip Khan daily. The cut he had taken from the King's sword had finally healed, but left a long thin scar atop his other scars. He wore no shirt as he was dragged to the whipping post. His old shirt was torn to shreds both from the whip and the guardsmen.

The warmth of spring was finally arriving and the prince was using that to his advantage. Many citizens of the kingdom were forced to watch and endure Khan's brutal and unmerciful torture.

Khan could see several townsfolk shrieking and crying, begging for Khan to be released every time the whip hit. The guardsmen made him stand just outside of the shade of the arena.

Even with the exhaustion setting in from the sun and relentless heat of the day, Khan couldn't help but let out a sick laugh as the prince came up slowly beside him. The prince's face showed no emotion, no feeling.

"Who is the girl to you?" Asked the prince as he gazed out into the sun drenched arena.

When Khan wouldn't give an answer, the prince punched him in the gut. He coughed and hunched over, only to be pulled up to face the prince by his hair.

"My father would like to know. If you would be so kind as to tell me." Whispered the prince in Khan's ear.

Khan chewed his lip and sniffed back a sigh as tears burned in his eyes.

"She's my sister. Her name is... mm... it's Drea."

❄❄❄

Khan collapsed to the floor of his cell in the King's mighty castle in a sweaty, bloody heap. He had fought with all his might. He could do no more; he could take no more. He was beaten. The prince had been hard and constant, he never seemed to falter, not once. Not even after the blows he suffered to his stomach, where Khan kicked, punched, jabbed, and slammed him in retaliation. Still the prince endured it all with no show of feelings. Khan thought this to be unnatural.

Khan slowly propped himself up on his knees and hands, only to have Malakai slide deftly past him and thrust a knee into his bruised and swollen face. Khan groaned and wretched as blood clogged his dry throat. Khan's instincts kicked in just as the prince came down to him. The prince was done with niceties. A knife stopped inches away from

Khan's left eye. With the prince being above him, he had the better advantage, but Khan was a lot younger. Khan had a bigger build than the prince. Surely, Khan could beat this miserable runt? Something inside him gave him hope and determination.

Khan's thoughts were driven away as the prince pulled a second knife and thrust it toward Khan's side. Khan dodged the blow as best he could, but the knife connected with the spot where the wounds on his back were from the whipping post. The wounds that had semi-healed were now bleeding once more. He grunted and struggled to keep the knife at bay. Khan wrestled with the prince, causing him to let go of the second knife.

In an instant, Khan had shoved the prince off of himself and mustered up the strength to stand. Not nearly a second or two after Khan stood, the prince's free hand struck him on the side of his jaw. Again, Khan fell to his knees, unable to take anymore. He jerked as the prince came around with a long, heavy chain and wrapped it quickly around Khan's throat.

His breath became labored as he pulled desperately at the tightening chains. In extreme pain, Khan knew he had to do something quick. He was running out of options. There was only one thing left to do. Maybe, all he had to do was talk?

He choked on his spit as his body began to jerk for air. Khan tapped rapidly on the prince's hands, in the hope he'd let Khan go so he could get a breath. A few seconds went by, making Khan believe the prince was indeed going to kill him.

But to his surprise, the prince reluctantly began to loosen the chains and then suddenly ripped them off his neck. Khan fell to the floor, gasping for air as he heard the prince pacing restlessly around the room. "Well? I'm waiting!"

❄❄❄

Khan knelt on the throne room floor, tiredly gazing at the King as he tried to process what Khan had just told him. Khan felt guilty for ratting Cordelia out and about telling them what was going to happen at one of the King's palaces.

Everything in his body ached and burned as Khan waited for the king to finish talking to his son. He caught very little of their conversation.

"Let her... Upper hand... Use that little dragon of yours..."

Khan watched the prince stand up straight and began to leave the throne. A look of disdain and anger was on the prince's face. The King shouted after his son,

"Do not hesitate!"

"Come, boy, you shall see what it takes to be a King." The King growled at Khan while he walked quickly by.

❄❄❄

Khan stumbled to a halt beside the King, unsure of what the King wanted to show him.

"Now, you've heard the rumors about me. The whispers of my dragon dying by my hand." Said the King, a hard, angry rasp clinging to his voice. "I planted those to hide this. Prepare yourself, my boy."

Khan looked at the King, unaware that what he would soon see would scar him for eternity. The King drew back a large orange curtain, revealing a massive door. The King unlocked the lock and swung the great door open to reveal one fiery green eye looking back at Khan.

Almost at once, Khan looked away as he saw the horrifying face of a dragon.

"Look. Look, boy!" Shouted the King.

Khan clenched his jaw, steadied himself, then looked up. Half of the dragon's face was exposed dirty, brown bone, while the other half was black and green, making the features of its face look sharp and harsh.

The *Dragon Slayer* never did kill his dragon. Khan felt sickened when he saw the hot ooze dripping from its fangs as it looked down at him. The dragon let out a gentle rumble that echoed in Khan's chest.

"She is the *Black Death*. Her name is Nishaeda." Whispered the King in fascination while rubbing his hand down the dragon's monstrous leg.

This monstrous beast had definitely endured countless battles and possibly just as many beatings. There were so many scars, some even held the shaft of an arrow still sticking out of its flesh.

Khan had to look away. The poor beast looked to have suffered greatly, just as he had. She looked as if she could be older than the earth itself.

Chapter II

A Taste of Fire

"You have not looked when we have asked you to. For this, we cannot show the whole truth."

Drea gaped at the blind dragon in disbelief. How could they not tell her what she and others must do to fulfill the prophecy? The Dragon Tarragōns were the ones Drea was speaking to. The prophecy they spoke of was that of the dragon egg that Khan had found.

"You have blocked us out when you needed to let us in. Child, greater things than you knowing everything, are at stake."

Drea hung her head in acceptance as the vision began to melt away.

She sighed ruefully then opened her eyes. It was odd that neither the prince nor his soldiers had been in to punish or torture her. It had allowed her the pleasure of some peace. She hoped they would at least leave Damion alone.

He looked to be doing worse than she was when she had last seen him. Her cuts and wounds had already started to heal. They had given her some cold water and a rag to clean up with. It felt so good to dab the cold water along her arms, neck and face. Her hair, however, would have to wait a while to be cleaned. It was a mass of thick, dirty, tangled black hair.

Drea had no inkling how long she had been in this murky cell, but it felt like months, even though it probably had only been a week or so. Her thoughts were pulled away from her tattered appearance as her stomach let out a giant rumble in protest for food.

She sighed and shut her eyes once more, the only thing she was allowed to eat was the stale dry bread that they pushed through her cell door once a day. As her thoughts wondered, she heard the creak of her cell door opening and the click of boots. Drea let herself breathe naturally. The steps got closer and she couldn't help but twitch when she heard whoever was there let out a hard sigh. Then a loud clunk of metal hit the floor, causing Drea to open her eyes and look back at the door. She looked in disbelief at the back of the guard that had tried to take her life walking toward her cell door.

He stepped out of her cell and closed the door behind him. She looked at what he had left on her floor. It was a fresh slice of bread and a thick cut of buttered and smoked beef. Her mouth watered as she picked up the plate with shaking hands.

Drea jumped as she heard a loud slam of a door in the distance. *What was that all about?* She thought. Right now, she didn't care, her hunger won over her thoughts. She stared at the plate and began eating the delicious meal.

❄❄❄

Rain poured down unforgivingly. Drea and Damion had somehow managed to escape with the help of Cordelia. Cordelia had set the armory on fire, diverting all of the prince's forces. Something happened that had allowed Damion to escape to his cell. Drea let out a short scream as the slippery mud took her feet out from under her. Damion, who was a short ways in front of her, slid to a halt and ran back to her and helped her up. They both slipped and slid through the mud and rain, trying to get as far away from their captors as possible.

They stopped at the gate, unsure of where to go next. Drea scanned the area, waiting for the appearance of guards and soldiers, while Damion looked for a way of transportation. Drea momentarily zoned out as a vision shifted through her head.

In that instant, she was shoved forward into the mud. She quickly looked back, the gate was shut, and Damion was on the other side of it. She jumped up and grabbed at his hands. Time slowed as a lean figure came up behind him. Malakai.

She screamed when she saw him thrust a sword through Damion's stomach. As Damion fell, she fell with him. His face hit the bars as he clutched his stomach. The blood flowed over and between his fingers until it pooled at his feet.

"No, no, no. Please, no..." She cried as she watched his eyes drain of life.

"Run" Was the final word he said before he slipped into unconsciousness.

Tears flowed from her eyes as everything went dark.

❄❄❄

Drea woke with a start, the dream she had just dreamed swiftly left her with no memory of it. She felt troubled but could not put her finger on the reason.

She sat up as daylight flooded into the room from the paneless window. She sighed, she knew this fight was far from over, whether hers ended now or later. Drea couldn't help but wish that it would end sooner.

Drea bowed her head and sent a silent prayer to the sky for the well-being of Khan. She really did hope he was alright. She opened her eyes and brought a knee to her chest as she pressed her back against the cell wall.

She clenched her jaw tightly when four men walked through her cell door. She slowly reached behind her back and gripped the knife that the guard had discarded after the prince stopped him from trying to kill her. She had taken it and hid it.

Drea could hurt people without any weapon, now that she was fully healed and well rested. She could be lethal to some with a weapon, no matter the size. She stood as the largest man stopped in front of her. Before he could say a word, she roared and lunged herself into the guards.

The next thing she knew, she was lying on the floor, her blood spilling onto the floor from the knife jammed into her left thigh. Her breath came in rugged gasps as she watched the two remaining men pull away the other two wounded men from her cell. Drea glanced at her thigh, the knife stuck out like a stone in a stream. She bit her lip as hard as possible, she knew it had to come out. She groaned as she made a circle with her fingers around the knife. She didn't pull it, she didn't have the courage. But she knew if she left it, it would just cause more damage.

Drea shivered as she squeezed the skin around the wound tightly. Exhaustion streamed over her as the last rays of the sun died out. The room was dark, murky and humid as she shut her eyes in pain.

❄❄❄

Drea! Drea, wake up!" Shouted a voice, waking Drea with an unwelcome start.

"Come on! Wake up!"

Drea jerked as the speaker slapped her across the cheek. She sighed when she saw Damion crouched in front of her, his face a mask of concern. She glared at him and said,

"Did you just slap me?"

Damion let out a short laugh and nodded. "I didn't know what else to do. You wouldn't wake up."

Drea nodded, furrowing her brow at him as she gazed at the open cell door.

"One of the stupid guards forgot his keys on his stool right by my door." Explained Damion as he noted her confusion.

She nodded slowly and looked him over. He seemed to be eating a lot better than her, there were no bruises or cuts on him at all.

"Now, come on, we need to get out of here while we still can. The armory is on fire. I don't know how it happened but it is and it's our chance to get out of this place."

"Wait, I can't walk, I have a knife in my leg." Murmured Drea to Damion as he stood up and started to walk away from her.

Damion glanced back at her and shook his head in disagreement.

"No, you don't."

Drea inspected her thigh, he was right, the knife was no longer there. She groaned as she stood up stiffly, with the help of Damion and they were off.

❄❄❄

The two ran as fast as they could through the empty corridors and halls. Where was everyone? The soldiers and guards were not at their stations. As Drea limped along, she saw a fine set of doors at the end of a hallway she was going opposite from. *Must be the prince's chambers,* she thought. The doors were decorated with fine silver and gold. Drea realigned her focus as Damion shouted at her when two guards turned the corner in front of them and cut them off. They were on them in an instant.

Damion grabbed a rather odd looking pole and swung it sideways. Drea grabbed hold of the other side of the pole and the two charged forward. She couldn't help but feel a twinge of guilt when they forced the guards down a flight of steps. She tried to shut out their painful shouts and grunts as they went tumbling down the steps.

"Come on!" Yelled Damion, latching onto her hand and tugging her down the steps after the two tumbling guards. Once at the bottom of the stairs, Drea yelled in surprise as one of the guards grabbed her foot while she was stepping over him.

Damion, instinctively, kicked the poor soldier in the face, knocking him out in an instant. Drea grunted as she was pulled away, through a large set of doors and into the courtyard. Damion turned his head toward the gate. Through the pouring rain, Drea could barely make out the figure of the prince standing in between them and the gate. Soldiers had them surrounded. Damion stood beside her, frozen. Lightning struck, illuminating each soldier facing them, their helmets were in the shape of a boar's head.

Drea's ears perked up as she heard the prince murmur, "Be my guest." and gestured with his hand.

In a flash, fire erupted above, making a line to where Drea and Damion couldn't cross. She looked at Damion, his eyes flashed heavy with fear and sorrow. They had no choice but to fight their way through. Time seemed to stand still. The prince ordered his men to charge. Drea braced herself, mustering up every ounce of courage she had left. This was it, maybe the final battle she'd have to fight.

She drew a breath, closed her eyes and allowed herself a moment of peace. Memories flashed through her mind as the sounds of thunder, and the violent clanking of armor reached through the muffled barrier and into her ears.

When she opened her eyes, she immediately flinched away, dodging a large ball of water that hit several of the soldiers that were dashing towards them. Cordelia! Could it be? Swiftly the young dragon came into view. She let out another round of water onto the rumbling fire in front of the gate so that it flickered out.

"Come on! Now's our chance!" Yelled Damion dashing toward the gateway.

Damion glanced around quickly for some ways of transportation. Drea retreated and watched as Cordelia quickly picked several of the soldiers off. The dragon let out a defeated roar as the prince's dragon came barreling down on her.

"You must find where one remains."

Uttered a voice in her head, Drea gasped and grabbed her head with her hands, eyes closed tightly. Visions of desert plains and volcanoes rumbled through her mind.

"Seek him out, red of dirt, brisk of fire."

In an instant, she was shoved forward into the mud. She glanced back, the gate was shut. Damion was on the other side of it. She jumped up and grabbed his hands. Time slowed as she recalled the dream she had. The same events were unfolding before her as a lean figure came up behind Damion.

Khan! She couldn't recall the last time she had felt such relief. She let out a laugh, it was cut off as lightning struck and lit up his face. Anger, hatred, and murder glittered in his eyes, his brow furrowed menacingly.

She screamed as she saw him thrust a sword through Damion's belly. As Damion fell, she fell with him. His face hit the bars. Damion pressed his hands to his stomach. The blood flowed over and between his fingers until it pooled at his feet.

"No. Why?! No! Please, no..." She cried as she watched his eyes drain of life.

"Run!"

She hissed in pain and sadness as Khan swiped at her. The tip of the sword caught her cheek. Tears fell and continued to fall as Drea got up, turned and ran as fast as she could away from the gate. The hurt and pain, she would never be able to forget. Her heart burned and ached as she sobbed and screamed to the wind. Why? Why did her brother... her only family, slaughter someone she had cared for?

Khan would have to pay dearly for what he has done, nothing he could say would make her forget what had just taken place. As Drea ran, she recalled the vision that made her oblivious to the world when another voice echoed in her head.

"Go to the barren wasteland that they call the 'Dead Lands'.

There you will find him."

Drea's heart sank with pain and fear. She would have to go where she never thought she'd go, not once in her entire life.

She'd have to go to the *Tailte Marbh.*

www.ingramcontent.com/pod-product-compliance
Ingram Content Group UK Ltd.
Pitfield, Milton Keynes, MK11 3LW, UK
UKHW021907190726
13853UKWH00002B/550